Grace sat ⟨...⟩
trying to s⟨...⟩

Her hand still ⟨...⟩
contact with ⟨...⟩
trying to show off. ⟨...⟩
mad.

He didn't think she was capable. In fact, he thought she was going to lose it any minute. Well, she aimed to prove him wrong.

She thought she was ready when he knocked on the door, but when she opened it she had to catch her breath. Jordan was dressed in a tight black T-shirt with the ATF logo embossed on the right-hand side, his biceps bulging just below the hem of the short sleeves. His hair was mussed and he had a hint of beard stubble lightly shadowing his jaw. But the *coup de grâce* was the sinfully tight jeans that showed off the heavy, thick muscles in his thighs.

Somehow her life had turned into an action-adventure flick when she wasn't looking. And the leading man was Jordan Kelly.

★ ★ ★

Dear Reader,

Lots of times things come full circle. I began my writing career with the Intimate Moments line, now called Romantic Suspense. My first book was published in 1997 and it was a thrill. Now after thirteen years, I'm back doing what I love to do—writing heart-pounding suspense!

That's what I have in store for you with *Five-Alarm Encounter*. Firefighter Grace Addision has been both physically and emotionally scarred by an arsonist who is stalking the people of La Rosa, California. She's on disability and recuperating when the mayor asks her to be part of the task force. She meets Jordan Kelly, the hard-hitting ATF agent who is the current task-force leader. Jordan knows she's not one hundred percent fit for the job, but that doesn't stop the sparks from flying between them. They must work together to stop not only the threat to the city, but the arsonist who has now targeted Grace. It's a race against time to keep both the city and her safe.

Full circle feels pretty darn good. I hope that you enjoy each intense and romantic moment!

All the best,

Karen Anders

KAREN ANDERS

Five-Alarm Encounter

ROMANTIC

SUSPENSE

Recycling programs
for this product may
not exist in your area.

ISBN-13: 978-0-373-27728-5

FIVE-ALARM ENCOUNTER

Books by Karen Anders

Harlequin Romantic Suspense

Five-Alarm Encounter #1658

KAREN ANDERS

is a three-time National Readers' Choice Award finalist and *RT Book Reviews* Reviewers' Choice finalist, and has won the prestigious Holt Medallion. Two of her novels made the Waldenbooks bestseller list in 2003. Published since 1997, she currently writes romantic suspense for Harlequin. To contact the author, please write to her in care of Harlequin Books, 233 Broadway Suite 1001, New York, NY 10279, or visit www.karenanders.com.

To Pete for always getting what I'm talking about *and* making it better!

Chapter 1

She couldn't breathe.

Grace Addison gasped for breath inside her mask. The explosion hit them so hard they were thrown across the room, slamming into an already unsteady staircase that had collapsed under their weight. They lay in the belly of the fire, smoke so thick Grace could barely see her surroundings.

Her mind screamed at her to do *something*. It demanded action from her like some cruel, unfeeling boss. Richard was dead. Grace knew it just by looking at him. Her paramedic training shouted at her to go to him, but she couldn't move.

Mind reeling, she turned her eyes away from the scene, trying to keep herself from weeping in horror. She focused on one thing. Sara, who was still alive, needed her.

From where Grace lay, she could see Sara's pleading

eyes peering through the clear, Plexiglas mask. Her best friend and fellow firefighter stared at Grace, beseeching her to help. Grace tried to make her body move, but she recognized the signs of shock. She cursed her weakness, her heart twisting with fresh pain, the oath she took as a firefighter going sour, like wine left too long to ferment.

The smoke was a dark, oppressive thing, weighing her down as if it had density. Mass.

Her lungs felt scorched. Orange and crimson flames crawled down the brown paneling toward them, their unrelenting journey consuming everything in their path.

She wanted to cry out. To scream for help, shout curses, *anything*. The clothes on Richard's body were starting to smoke. Grace struggled against panic. Her slightest movement brought a searing pain across her back. She froze, immobilized by the fierce sensations that racked her with shocking intensity.

Richard was burning!

The couch and shag carpet nearby were consumed in smoke. A wall tapestry was wreathed in flames and hissed audibly as it melted away. She coughed, tears flowing freely from eyes that stung excruciatingly.

They lay there as the fire encroached. Grace could hear the sound of movement above her. She tried to call out, to scream for their rescue. But her throat was parched. She could barely get a sound beyond the smothering mask.

A short, audible beep emitted from her Personal Alert Safety System. The device was warning her that she'd been immobile for more than thirty seconds. She was relieved at the warning and the 95-decibel tone that sounded shortly afterward. Every part of her was riveted on Sara's eyes, giving her friend that small amount of comfort as she slowly suffocated.

The scorching heat on Grace's back and shoulders intensified, telling her the barrier of her turnout coat had been breached, but again, she couldn't focus on it. Just on Sara. Her world had narrowed down to Sara.

Frantically, Sara pulled off the mask, gasping in the tainted basement air. She reached out for Grace's hand and Grace grasped it tightly, their gazes locked. Grace squeezed and Sara's eyes welled with tears. It was almost like Sara was trying to say something. Her hand contorted and jerked, then her eyes went fixed and still, her mouth going slack.

A flood of genuine tears washed away some of the sting of the smoke as Grace's vision began to dim. Her lungs felt compressed with agony as she struggled for oxygen. The red-hot pain increased along her back and shoulders, the smell of charred skin thick in her nostrils.

She was going to die.

Grace woke up gasping and choking. She threw the covers off, feeling as though her back and shoulders were on fire. She stumbled to the window and jerked it open. The cool air from the La Rosa night wafted into the room, easing some of Grace's panic and soothing her hot shoulders and back. She braced herself against the windowframe, breathing in the chill for a moment, as grateful as if she'd just been saved from drowning.

There was no more burned flesh there, nothing but scars now. But the internal scars from that day were fresh and oozing.

The serial arsonist had struck again, planted a slowly ticking time bomb in a residential building. Only one of the many fires he had set, hoping to claim more victims. This time the greedy flames had taken two of the department's best.

Grace squeezed her eyes tightly together, trying to block out Sara's beautiful blue eyes fixed in death.

The memory was as fresh now as it had been two months ago. It haunted her. Pursued her. Stalking. Accosting. No matter how hard she tried to block it out, she couldn't escape. She relived that horrible experience within the recesses of her mind like a cruelly conducted interrogation.

At least she was alive, but that meant living with the memory. Guilt assaulted her waking and sleeping. Her colleagues had gotten to her in time.

How could a residential fire in a three-story house have gone so bad? Their station had been the first to respond, but more stations had been called in as the fire escalated to a three alarm.

Her turnout coat had protected her from most of the damage of the fire, but when Grace looked in the mirror, her ravaged flesh was a scarred reminder that she'd almost lost her life.

She looked at her bedside clock; the illuminated numbers read 4:00.

Unable to go back to sleep, Grace sank down to the floor near the open window and breathed in deep of the cool air that drifted across her face.

After a moment of deep breathing, the night called to her and she reached for her running gear. She ran from the nightmares. She ran to feel in control again, but the fear was always there, just a few steps behind.

She made her way along the dirt path overlooking a still-slumbering La Rosa—the city that was under her charge as a firefighter, the city she'd sworn to protect.

Had she failed?

Her back and shoulders felt tight.

The burns were a permanent reminder of the fire that had damaged her flesh.

Her breathing hitched. Such a simple act—breathing in and breathing out. Until you couldn't; until your breath was strained and the oxygen replaced by toxic chemicals that sucked the life from you in a slow, helpless suffocation.

Rocks crunched beneath her feet as she neared the apex of the trail. It opened up, widening into a path that wound back down the corkscrew pass. At the top, she stopped, as she always did, and looked down at the city nestled northeast of San Diego's sprawling metropolis.

The sun was just starting to rise, streetlights winked off and traffic flowed. Her breathing slowed and leveled out. Sweat ran in rivulets down her back and her arms. She swiped at her forehead with a terry wristband as the sweat stung her eyes.

As the sun rose in the east, it bathed the city of about two hundred thousand citizens in a soft, rosy glow, accentuating the red-tiled, Spanish-inspired roofs. She could see all the way into the revitalized downtown. Any tourist would think La Rosa's renovation was a beautifully planned project that changed the face of the old and new architecture, giving it a much-needed face-lift, but Grace saw potential targets, potential hazards that could at any moment burst into flame by an arsonist's hand.

The edge of McCaffrey Park—a five-hundred-acre jewel that extended to the base of the foothills—was only a couple of blocks away.

Was that a plume of smoke in the distance? Her

breath stumbled to nothing and held. Did it curl up into the sky with deadly intent?

Her breathing increased, but it wasn't the steady breathing of a good, healthy run. She knew, even before she tried to stop it, that she was hyperventilating.

She turned away and ran at a breakneck pace down the steep slope, her heart pounding, her senses on full alert, like a terrified deer. At the bottom, she tripped and lost her footing, falling to the ground with a hard thump, scraping her knee and the palms of her hands as she braced for the impact.

For a moment, she lay in the dirt and let the panic wash over her. Finally, she summoned enough control to push it away, push it someplace else.

Slowly, she pulled herself back up and brushed herself off.

She looked once again to the place where she thought she had seen the smoke and realized there wasn't anything there.

No fire.

For a moment, she stood there, acknowledging she had overreacted. Her sense of duty warring with her terrible fear. But her *duty* right now was to get well. There were others who were responsible for the protection of La Rosa.

She was recuperating.

She stopped and looked back at the city, still below her. Something dark and twisted had settled there. That thing had touched her.

An arsonist was causing murder and mayhem. He had killed two of her colleagues.

But she had survived.

Just barely.

And the arsonist was still out there.

* * *

Back at her house, she took her shower as usual, ignoring the roughness of her skin where it met the sloping line of her shoulders. She tried to shrug off the dream that replayed the reality of that day.

She had to shake this…this self-pity and fear. After exiting the shower, she stared at herself in the mirror. She looked the same as she had before. She had the same big blue eyes, the same slightly curly, long blond hair. She couldn't resist a morbid urge to glance at the reflection of her shoulders as she began to dress.

But it wasn't just her self-image that had been changed that day. The trauma of watching Sara die was something Grace couldn't shake. It was like she'd been watching her own death and now she was living some kind of weird out-of-body experience.

She knew that wasn't true, but she couldn't seem to reconnect.

The harsh ringing of her cell broke her concentration and startled her. With her heart pounding, she flipped it open.

"Grace Addison?" a voice asked on the other end of the line.

"Yes, this is Grace."

"This is Tim Dawson in the mayor's office. The mayor would like to meet with you today at ten o'clock."

"What is this about?"

"The mayor will explain it all to you when you meet with him. Is ten o'clock convenient, Ms. Addison?"

"Yes, that will be fine," Grace said softly. She disconnected the call, bewildered as to what the mayor of La Rosa wanted to speak with her about.

Was he was worried that she would sue?

All three of the self-contained breathing apparatuses—

or, as firefighters called them, SCBAs—they were wearing the day Richard Moore and Sara Parker died may have been faulty. Unfortunately, the effects of the explosion and the fall could have damaged the equipment, so the findings were inconclusive.

Grace had no interest in suing the city. She had simply needed the time to heal and recuperate, and her benefits had taken care of both her medical expenses and her time off from the La Rosa Fire Department.

Turning her attention to dressing, she chose her garments carefully. The white blouse covered her scars, and the black pencil skirt hugged her hips. Hips that were not as generous as they used to be. Grace made a mental note to eat more.

She walked down the wooden stairs and through the house she had worked hard to renovate and decorate. But it all seemed so inconsequential to her now.

She grabbed the banister, the wood smooth beneath her palm. She remembered when Sara had helped her to sand every inch of it. They were supposed to paint it the very next weekend. Now it was a daily reminder that Sara would never apply varnish to the lovingly restored wood. Grace paused before going outside, sweeping the room with a quick glance. She rarely even visited this part of the house anymore, save for leaving. It seemed as though Sara's presence was here sometimes, drifting through with tasks left undone.

Opening the front door, she paused. Lying on her welcome mat was an envelope—a plain, brown nine-by-twelve envelope.

Automatically, she looked around for whoever could have left it. The hair on the back of her neck stood up. Cautiously, she dipped down and picked it up. It had no writing on the outside. With fingers that had suddenly gone clumsy, she opened the clasp. She tilted the envelope and let some of the contents slide out into her hand. Grace's eyebrows drew together as she stared down at a handful of eight-by-ten photographs that seemed to have been taken in poor lighting conditions. A sudden realization of what they were coursed through her body like an electric shock. Her frame shook violently and her breath wrenched into a gasp. She saw Richard lying recumbent on the floor, his body yet unburned. There was Sara, too, looking tortured and dying behind her mask. And, she saw herself, helpless, already on fire, her hand reaching out to her friend.

She cried out loud as her shocked eyes fell on the pictures of that fateful day. Pictures that could only have been taken by the arsonist.

A fury, the likes of which she'd never experienced before, engulfed her and she released a broken sob. She flipped through each photo faster and faster, her shocked gaze riveted to the last agonizing moments of Sara's life grotesquely caught and frozen in time. Each picture she looked at only increased the panic that started in her gut and twisted up through flesh and bone into something almost seething with malice.

She backpedaled into the house and slammed the door. The photos fell from her suddenly numb hands, scattering onto the floor of the foyer. Grace backed away from them, her back hitting the door with a thud.

She closed her eyes against the knowledge that he'd somehow taken pictures using some kind of remote camera and watched the whole incident play out. He never made a move to help or rescue them.

He killed Richard.

He *let* Sara die.

He would have let her die, too.

Fear gripped her and her breathing increased, her heart pounding from the adrenaline that pumped into her system. Tears filled her eyes as she bent down and quickly picked up all the pictures, her hands trembling with rage. She began to shove them all back in the envelope, but discovered something else inside.

A single sheet of paper with block letters on it read, "You didn't escape. Flames are patient. They know your name. They wait for you, Grace." It was signed, "Vulcan."

She gritted her teeth, a feeling of dread washing over her. She slid the paper back into the envelope and closed the clasp. With unsteady steps that grew firmer, she went into her kitchen to get a plastic bag and dropped the envelope into the protective covering.

She took a few moments to get control of herself. All she wanted to do was don her T-shirt and shorts and run off the jumbled, intense emotions clawing through her.

Still unsettled, she tucked the plastic bag into her purse. In case the bastard was skulking somewhere nearby, she made a determined effort to keep her features smooth and even. Grace got into her car and headed to her appointment.

A few minutes later she found herself inside the town hall and was soon ushered into the mayor's office.

The moment the door opened, Grace noticed the tall, muscular man, standing to the side of the mayor's desk, wearing an impeccable blue suit.

Who was he? A high-powered attorney?

The man turned when the door opened and Grace got the full force of his intense eyes, the color of the sea. Her heart suspended in her chest at the sheer impact of his handsome, movie-star looks. Any woman would pause admiringly when faced with such awesome male beauty.

In the past, she might have smiled and flirted subtly, confident and sure in her own skin. Resisting the urge to rub at her scars, she pushed away the unbidden thought that she was now damaged goods. She knew it was irrational, but she couldn't help it. Once the initial shock of meeting him faded, Grace noticed that those deep blue eyes held quite a bit of hostility and she realized that it was directed toward her.

She had to wonder how she'd stepped on his toes when she didn't even know him.

Not understanding the situation she'd just walked into, Grace ignored the man and focused on the mayor. Greg Baker had the perfect politician's face and knew how and when to manipulate people.

The mayor rose and smiled, motioning Grace forward and offering her a seat. Grace walked toward the desk and noticed the man watching her cross the room.

"Grace, what a pleasure to see you again. You look well." The mayor offered his hand and Grace shook it.

"Let me introduce you to our resident ATF agent, Jordan Kelly. He's been helping us with the arson investigation and was instrumental in setting up the task force. He's an excellent leader."

Great. A know-it-all fed.

Grace turned to Jordan. Standing this close to him set off detonations along her skin. The dark blue suit fit him to a tee, accentuating his broad shoulders and wide chest before tapering down to a flat stomach. He stepped closer to her and her breathing deepened as she took in the scent of him—crisp and clean.

"Yes, but it seems the mayor plans on making a bit of a change."

His words were laced with animosity, and he scrutinized her with those cutting eyes of his.

He reached out to shake her hand. When he brought his hand back to his side, she noticed that he made a fist as if trying to dispel the energy that had crackled between them.

"What change is that?" she asked.

"Well," Greg said, "I want you to co-lead the group with Jordan."

Grace swung around to face Greg, her eyes wide. "What? You want me to join the task force?"

"Yes. You were about to finish out your arson training and worked under the best we had. You know this arsonist."

"Yes," Grace said softly, looking away from Greg, but getting snagged by Jordan's gaze. Still hostile. She rubbed at the scars on the back of her shoulder. "I know him."

Those intense blue eyes studied her intently, as if he couldn't quite believe that she was being asked to do this. For her part, she didn't even feel remotely ready to take on any responsibility.

"You want me to co-lead with Agent Kelly?"

"Yes, he's got excellent instincts and was formally with the FBI. You will share the duties and leadership, as I said."

"I haven't been cleared for active duty. I'm still on disability at the moment."

"I took the liberty of clearing this with your boss, Grace. I understand if you feel you aren't up to it. But we need you, Grace. With your knowledge, you'd be invaluable in securing an arrest along with obtaining justice for your fellow firefighters who were murdered in cold blood. Surely you wouldn't want to fail them and the citizens of La Rosa?"

Guilt stabbed through her like a double-edged knife, her heart twisting with fresh pain. She bit her lip, fury at what that bastard had done by so callously standing there and simply watching as they died.

It was clear to her that the mayor was manipulating her emotions, but it didn't diminish the strong feelings that coursed through her.

Grace also realized that her appointment to the task force would garner good press. The only surviving firefighter from that devastating La Rosa house fire now part of the task force to apprehend the bastard who was torching residential areas. The monster that had almost taken her life and had left her scarred, that had branded the memory of the terror and the pain deep into her very tissue.

Grace had to admit that she wanted to catch the man who had killed a dozen people, including funny and dedicated Rick and sweet and caring Sara.

It didn't take much for her to make up her mind. But it would be best to reveal that she herself was now being stalked. She pulled the envelope out of her purse and held it up.

Jordan looked at it with narrowed eyes. "What's that?"

"It's a threat from the arsonist. He's not done with me."

"May I?" he asked, reaching out for the envelope. Grace handed him the plastic-covered package. The brush of her skin was like a lick of flame. It was unprofessional and inappropriate, but he justified his reaction to her because a man had to be dead or seriously dysfunctional not to react to this woman. She had a shimmering, fragile beauty that brought out a man's protective instincts.

Jordan Kelly had a good solid mad going, and he didn't want to feel any sympathy for Grace Addison. She was here to make his job more difficult. The mayor was playing politics.

So the mayor brings in the only surviving victim of the arsonist who was plaguing the town of La Rosa. Damn politicians.

He set the envelope down on the edge of the mayor's desk, slipping on gloves. Very carefully he unwrapped the package and opened the clasp.

There in vivid color was the harrowing incident Grace had survived. Three firefighters lay in a heap next to each other. Debris and smoke circled in the air. It was clear that Richard Moore was dead. The way he was positioned bore out the autopsy report that he had broken his back when he'd been flung across the room and hit the unstable stairs. The stairs had given way and the three of them had landed on the hard concrete of the basement floor.

That was a long fall. He glanced at Grace, whose heavily lashed, beautiful blue eyes were fixed on the photos, her skin white.

This fragile woman had fallen so far and survived dwindling air supply from a faulty or critically damaged SCBA. Sara Parker hadn't been so lucky.

Jordan's mouth tightened when he got to the note. He swung his eyes to Grace. But Grace was no longer there. She was back in that basement, reliving that incident. Her breathing was shallow, her skin even paler. As much as he didn't want to sympathize with the woman taking his job, no one could view those photos and not feel compassion for the woman who had endured such an ordeal. The way she looked right now in the throes of her memory would haunt him for a long time.

It was a look he often saw on his own face when he glanced in the mirror, a look prompted by his own memories.

Abruptly, Grace said, "I'll do it. I'll be part of the task force."

His mouth tightened. Surely, this had to be a joke. She wasn't fit to take this job. She wasn't ready to be back to work on a case that was just too close to her. Greg Baker was an idiot and he'd manipulated Grace into taking the position for his own damn gain. Jordan grudgingly had to admit the woman had courage.

Didn't mean he thought she was right for the job, though. Didn't mean he thought she should be given any leadership role. He was a trained ATF agent and he could lead this team without her.

"I should enter this into evidence."

"*We* should," she said firmly. "I'd also like to be brought up to speed about the investigation to date."

He put the pictures and the note back into the envelope with care and then slipped it back into its protective plastic bag. She was already issuing orders.

"By all means," he said as he gave the mayor a loaded look of contempt. "Let's do that."

He walked ahead of her so he could open the door. She inclined her head and walked through. Jordan followed and couldn't help but notice the sexy way she walked, the swing of her hips, the soft, enticing curves of her very feminine body.

Damn, he'd been in the field too long.

They emerged from the town hall into the bright morning sunlight of a La Rosa summer.

"There's really no need to come with me to catalog this evidence, Grace."

"No, I'm sure you'd be happy if I simply disappeared."

After taking a few more steps, he realized she'd stopped walking. He turned around.

"Look, it's no secret I'm against your joining the task force. I'll admit it."

Walls slammed into place, a protective barrier that had probably served her well in the male-dominated world of firefighting. The fact that this delicate woman had passed all the tests and made it into one of the most dangerous jobs on the planet floored him.

"That's right. You've made that abundantly clear, Agent Kelly."

"It's Jordan. And it's clear to me you aren't fully healed."

Firecrackers went off in her eyes as they narrowed on him. He had to say he liked them better this way than with the fresh terror in them. She crossed her arms over her chest, a fully protective stance. It reinforced his sense that Grace was hiding some pretty strong emotions and issues behind those stunning eyes.

"How do you know whether or not I'm healed? Are you a doctor now, too?"

"No, I'm a war vet and a former FBI negotiator. I notice the signs."

"There are no signs, Agent Kelly," she said with conviction. "I refuse to be a victim. I refuse to hold back when I might be able to make a difference, bring this man to justice. He killed my friends. He's killed a dozen people."

"I'm not disputing your anger and need for justice,

Grace. I just don't need a liability when I'm trying to do my job."

Grace took the remaining steps between them, which almost put her at eye level. Her eyes were breathtaking this close up. Impossibly blue, shot with shards of pure gold and rimmed in black. They were snapping with barely contained anger…and vulnerability. How she managed to pull it off, he wasn't sure. She smelled enticing and decadent, like bottled sin, which sent his senses reeling.

"Well, I'm afraid in this case the best man for the job is a woman."

Those words brought him back to his senses and caused all his doubts and condemnations to surface. He was about to say something totally unprofessional when an explosion rent the air. The resulting concussion from the blast pushed him forward directly into Grace, but he was already moving in that direction anyway. They fell and he covered her body with his own, the reflex of a man who never thought of his own personal safety first.

Another explosion caused smoke and fire to geyser fifteen feet into the sky. The gas tank of her car exploded with a boom that he was sure could be heard for miles. His ears rang with the sound.

"Grace, are you hurt?"

Jordan spoke to her, but it was as if his words were trying to reach her through water. She was distracted by both the terrible explosion that made pain flare along her shoulders and neck, but was juxtaposed with the very comforting feel of Jordan's big, male body covering hers. His arms were around her and his serious and concerned face filled her vision. He kept her grounded in the here and now so she couldn't revert back to that fateful and terrible day.

"Grace?" Jordan said again, and then gently shook her. She could hear the pop and ping of burning metal. When she caught a glimpse of the flames, irrational fear and panic filled her. She cried out and reeled away from him, retreating to one of the thick pillars. Breathing heavily, she pressed her back against it, turning her face away from the carnage below her.

"Grace? Are you all right?"

It took everything she had to look at him and nod. His eyes were unreadable and assessing. Her stomach clenched in both anger and resentment. Who was he to judge her?

In the distance she could hear sirens. As they drew closer, she vowed he wasn't going to intimidate her. His look gave her what she needed to pull herself together. She pushed away from the pillar and straightened, her eyes hardening.

As one of the engines from her firehouse pulled up to the curb, Grace finally looked down to the street. Men and women jumped out of the truck, hooking up hoses and immediately getting a stream of water on the contorted metal that had once been a vehicle.

She mentally checked herself. She would be a bit bruised but, thankfully, that would be it.

Jordan rose to his feet as Fire Chief Michael Lawrence approached them.

"Are you two okay?" he asked, giving Grace a quick, furtive glance.

He motioned over a paramedic and the young, eager man made them sit down on the steps while he checked them out.

Grace met Jordan's eyes and he had that same

assessing look in them. She had better not give him any fuel with which to compromise her and get her removed from her new job.

"You're seriously being targeted by this guy. I think that puts us all in a precarious position."

"The destruction of my car is nothing but a warning. He's after me, not the team. I guarantee you I'm not going to cower and hide. He's not going to do that to me."

"You're going to face an uphill battle. The team isn't prepared for this change."

"They'll just have to accept it. I'm more than determined to do what I have to do to bring this monster to justice. I'll also do it with or without your cooperation. I understand why you resent me. No one likes to be told they're not doing a good job. But we both know this change in leadership is not fueled by your perceived lack of competence. It's purely political."

"Regardless of how it came about, we have to work together, Grace. It doesn't sit well with me under the circumstances, especially now that you've been targeted by this guy. Why is he fixated on you, do you think?"

"Do you know who Vulcan is?"

"The only Vulcan I know is Mr. Spock," Jordan said.

"Vulcan is the patron deity of alchemy, and he is symbolic of the hermetic art. The tenet is that nothing has been created as *ultima material,* which means the state of ultimate being. Everything is *prima material,* which is just ordinary, rough matter. But, when Vulcan is involved, the art of alchemy develops it into its final substance. The arsonist wants me to realize my potential by being exposed to the fire."

"So, on top of being a killer, he's a nutjob."

"Is that your professional opinion?" Grace asked.

Jordan smiled in reaction to the sarcasm in her voice. His eyes twinkled and her heart did a quick pitter-pat.

"My guess is he's the type who identifies with fire, who thinks it needs to be allowed free rein to do its work, someone who believes it shouldn't be contained."

"Yeah," Jordan said. "A nutjob."

Grace laughed unexpectedly, the sound almost alien to her. She couldn't remember the last time she'd actually laughed.

"Grace." Michael Lawrence's voice was filled with dread. "There's an envelope here for you."

The smile faded from her face and Grace rose, her chest suddenly tight. Her eyes darted to the hunk of ruined metal, then to a white envelope clearly visible on the stairs of the town hall.

"Do you have any gloves on you?"

Jordan pulled a pair out of his suit coat pocket and handed them to her. On shaking legs, she made her way down the last few steps and bent down to pick up the envelope.

With trembling fingers she carefully broke the seal. In block letters, the single sheet of paper read, "Just a reminder the flames wait for you, Grace. You cannot escape their embrace." It was signed, "Vulcan."

With a soft cry, Grace looked up once again at the charred, twisted metal.

Walking over to the heap of slag, she looked beneath it and saw the distinctive soda can MO, confirming her suspicion.

The "nutjob" had just sent her a very serious warning.

Chapter 2

"It looks like you're going to need protection, Grace," Jordan said.

She started to shake her head, but then realized he was right. She couldn't go back to her house. It wasn't safe for her or for anyone close by. Disoriented, Grace swayed on her feet. The trauma of the explosion and the presence of the flames had simply stolen her equilibrium.

Jordan's steadying hand on her arm grounded her for a moment.

Anger flared, bright and strong, making her jaw clench and her body stiffen. She wasn't going to give in to the weakness. She wasn't going to be a victim.

"I'll worry about that later. Right now, I want to get started on finding this maniac."

"No one would fault you for taking a day off to recover from this situation," Jordan said gently.

"Don't try to handle me, Agent Kelly. I can handle myself. I say we get these two pieces of evidence logged, and then you can brief me on the investigation to date."

His blue eyes flashed and contradicted her words. She couldn't disagree with him. She had broken down, but she was in control of herself now and she would remain that way. He was an appealing man, but it would be a mistake to think he wouldn't try anything to discredit her and get her removed from the task force. He was very handsome and, from what she gathered so far, very intelligent.

She shivered and was the first one to break eye contact. "If you would lead the way to your vehicle, Agent...Jordan, I would appreciate it. Mine won't get us across the street."

He sighed and said gruffly, "Come on. It's this way."

When he stopped in front of a black SUV, Grace snickered.

"What?" he asked.

"There's a reason feds are stereotyped on TV and in films."

He chuckled and said, "Get in and keep your snarky comments about my ride to yourself."

"Okay, if you insist," she said.

She settled herself in the passenger seat and secured her seat belt. Jordan got in and did the same. "We'll go to the police department and get this evidence cataloged, and then what do you say about some lunch while I brief you on the case?"

Her stomach rumbled at the mention of food.

"I'll take that as a yes."

"You know all this levity is going to tarnish your reputation as a hard-hitting fed."

He turned toward her and, in the close confines of the car, his magnetism was amplified. His dark, thick hair was just a tad too long to be considered regulation. His tie was a splash of crimson against the starched white shirt, and instead of wearing sensible shoes, he was wearing cowboy boots. He exuded confidence and a "Don't mess with me" attitude.

"Don't let that fool you, Grace. When I get serious, you'll know it."

Those words sent a shiver down her spine and settled like an electric shock in the pit of her stomach.

"Nice boots. Government issue?"

"Nope," he said, grinning. "Purely kick-ass."

Jordan Kelly was one tough guy, she had no doubt, a complicated, intriguing man who made her think more along the lines of law and disorder. She'd bet he knew how to disassemble a woman with ease. She'd have to be on her guard. Irrationally, she wondered how he would react to her scars, wondered if his perfect features would show his distaste at her imperfection, the evidence of her trauma.

When they pulled up to the precinct, Jordan led her into the sedate La Rosa Police Department. There wasn't much crime in the small city adjacent to San Diego— only an arsonist who was determined to destroy it.

The mayor was eager to bring this monster to justice, and Grace understood why. A lot of the tourists visiting San Diego would find their way to the quaint city that was well known for its artist community and antiques. If those tourist dollars dried up because of bad publicity, it could spell disaster for the city's economy.

But that was the mayor's worry. All Grace cared

about was finding the man who had so callously set that house fire and then watched his handiwork with relish.

"Grace?"

She started out of her reverie and blinked a couple times.

"What has you so preoccupied?"

"I was thinking about the reason the mayor decided to make me co-lead."

"Yeah, slimy politician. He's worried about money and his own ass. Same old story."

Grace followed Jordan past the front desk. She looked around, half wondering if Sara's husband, a beat cop, was on duty today.

"What's wrong?"

Startled by his voice, Grace looked into Jordan's eyes.

"Nothing," she lied.

"You look like a little kid peering furtively into a closet, worried you'll see the bogeyman."

"Sara's husband works here. She was one of the victims who died in the fire."

"Do you have a problem with him?"

"Possibly, but I can't think about that now."

"Why is he mad at you?"

"I can't shake the feeling that he somehow blames me for living and his wife dying."

Jordan stopped moving and turned to her. "You're kidding, right? I saw those photos, Grace. I know how far you fell and how the sheer force of that explosion could easily scramble your brains. You were running out of air and slowly suffocating. You were on fire, being burned." His eyes darted to her shoulders. "Surely, he's not going to hold a grudge."

Her breathing increased with each word he spoke and she knew he'd read the report. That was the only way he would have known she'd been on fire, that she had scars.

Mortified, she brushed past him and headed for the evidence room. "I didn't say it was rational," she murmured as she made a conscious effort to slow her breathing and tamp down the rising panic.

"True. He did lose a loved one, and that tends to make people...do things they normally wouldn't."

The tone of his voice alerted her to the fact that Jordan had some real-world experience with a grieving person. In his professional capacity perhaps?

Or was it personal?

It didn't matter. She wasn't going to get close enough to him to find out. He could keep his secrets and she'd keep hers.

When they got to the evidence room, Jordan filled out the necessary paperwork to get the photos and the notes cataloged as evidence. He left instructions for fingerprinting to be done, as well as analysis on the paper and the photos to see if that would give them any leads.

Jordan then brought her to the desk of Ray Russo.

The man in front of her had his head down, reading something on his desk. She saw baldness faintly gleaming through carefully combed-over gray hair.

"Grace, this is Ray, the lead detective on the task force. Ray, Grace Addison. She is joining us on the task force."

"As co-leader," she said.

"She's being stalked by the guy who has been starting fires. Calls himself Vulcan. He gave her two messages. She needs to get that documented and get some protection."

Ray cast her a scathing glance. His black eyes were unfriendly, glittering with much more hostility than Jordan's had when they first met. He heaved his bulk out of his chair to stand and clumsily shook her offered hand in his own oversized one. Before turning away to face Jordan, he absently wiped his hand on his side as if ridding himself of a pungent ooze.

"Vulcan? What is that? Who says?" His New York accent was thick and Grace wondered how long he'd been living in Southern California.

"Grace says that's what he calls himself."

"Whaa? She's being chased by a whole damn planet? Maybe she should see a shrink and stop watching old *Star Trek* reruns." He laughed heartily, a clumsy attempt to soften the words into a joke. When neither Jordan nor Grace responded, he said, "Well, little lady, take a seat and we'll get this done as quickly as we can without any fuss or muss."

She looked at Jordan as she took the chair and gave him a long-suffering look.

"It's no joke," Jordan replied. "She just had her car blown up outside town hall this morning. Matches the perpetrator's MO from what I could tell."

Ray's eyes widened and he turned his gaze on her. "Blew up your car? You sure it wasn't your driving? Ya know what they say—women drivers, no survivors!" Ray let out a chuckle.

Grace looked at the cop, shook her head. His blatant comments at her expense were too lowbrow to dignify with a response.

"What is important is that you weren't in it," Ray

continued. He spread his hands and gave a slight nod as if he thought he was the Fonz.

After the incident with the photos had been documented, Ray said, "Where will you be staying?"

"I don't know that yet."

He raised a brow and looked at Jordan. "Well, what you need to do here is protect her. Women need protection, being the weaker of the sexes." He smiled at her like a Cheshire cat.

Grace gritted her teeth. Better to swallow back her comments and remain calm in the wake of Ray's blatant chauvinism than lose it and show she wasn't fit for the leadership of the task force.

"Thank you, Detective Russo, for all your help."

He looked disappointed that she hadn't risen to the bait.

"What is up with that guy?" Grace asked after they left his desk.

"Ray is a chauvinistic jerk. He doesn't like it when women are in authority. He got burned by a woman boss in his past. He's harmless."

"My skin is thick enough, Jordan. Firefighting is normally considered a man's profession, so I'm used to it in the fire department. Just didn't know why he was being so hostile."

They left the precinct and Grace breathed a sigh of relief to have the prospect of running into Tom Parker, Sara's husband, behind her for now. She knew she would have to face him eventually.

She remembered how unsettled she'd been during Sara's service, with her healing burns still a searing mess. Her doctor had advised against her going, but Grace had been adamant. She wasn't going to miss either Sara's funeral or Richard's.

She owed them that much.

"La Rosa does have a damn fine diner. Mind if we go there?"

"No, I don't mind."

"Are you feeling better after this morning?"

"Aside from the fact that this nutjob, as you so eloquently put it, torched my vehicle and ousted me from my home? Sure. I feel great."

He chuckled, reached out and squeezed her shoulder. Grace jerked away to the other side of the car and Jordan swore softly under his breath.

"I'm sorry, Grace. Did I hurt you?"

"No, it doesn't hurt anymore. I was just caught off guard." Her sensitivity to her scars ran much deeper than she wanted to admit. Her reaction to Jordan's hand on her had been pure knee-jerk.

His touch had caused so much turmoil inside her. Part of it was her fear that he could feel the roughness of her scars. The other, more disturbing part was the way the warmth of his hand had penetrated her cotton shirt and caused a flurry of sensations in her stomach.

"I didn't mean to make you feel uncomfortable."

She nodded, just wanting to get past the awkward moment.

Jordan pulled up in front of the diner and they both got out of the highly charged atmosphere of the SUV. He held the door for her as she stepped inside the busy diner.

"We'd like a booth as soon as possible," he said to the hostess.

She nodded and gave him a warm smile. "Welcome back, Agent Kelly."

They only waited a few moments for a booth to open up.

"Grace…"

"Jordan, can we just agree to let it go?"

His features hardened and Grace recalled their conversation about her knowing when he was serious. Well, she could tell. He was dead serious now.

"No, I can't because you're now part of this team. You're not one hundred percent and you know it. Peoples' lives are on the line and you need to be fit for duty."

"It doesn't matter what you think. You're looking for any excuse you can find to get me booted off the team, but I'm as fit as I need to be. That's all you need to know."

"In this business, Grace, people who screw up die."

She turned to him, her voice low and severe. Jordan watched her with an unnerving intensity. "I know that. I lived through it." She wished she could erase the pictures in her head, the guilt that spiraled inside her like a living vortex that sucked at her equilibrium.

"I think you should be evaluated. Get some counseling." His features softened just a bit. "I have firsthand knowledge of what happens when an agent is not fit for duty."

Although she was curious about what had happened to him to give him such a grave and sad look in his eyes, she wasn't going to ask. She didn't want to bond with this man. Grace turned away. "This discussion is over. It's time to focus on how we're going to catch this bastard and put him behind bars. That's our job. Together, as a team."

She heard Jordan sigh as she moved away from him and entered the booth.

He stood there for a moment. Then with another sigh, he sat down across from her.

He saw too much. She'd hate to have him try to dig any deeper into her mind or the secrets that she kept… even from herself. Right now he was annoyed with her, but he'd leave her alone to do her job.

She hoped.

"Okay, let's pretend you are fine and dandy, then, Grace. I can't force you to do anything. The one in control here is the mayor and he's dead set on your being part of the task force."

She closed her eyes briefly. It had already been a long day. The ache of fatigue reached all the way down to her bones. "Thanks for your grudging vote of confidence, Agent Kelly. Now fill me in on what's been going on while I was recuperating."

The waitress interrupted before Jordan could respond. She turned over the cups with a rattle and filled them both with coffee. She was a gum-snapping, fresh-faced sixteen-year-old who looked like she didn't have a care in the world. Grace envied the girl her youthful innocence.

"What can I get for you?"

Grace had made a promise to herself that she would eat more. She ordered a club sandwich. One of the more calorie laden choices on the menu.

Jordan ordered a Reuben and the waitress left with a snap of her gum.

Grace eyed his trim figure. "Don't tell me you're one of those guys who can eat what he wants and not gain a pound."

Jordan snorted and poured cream in his coffee. "Nope. I run to keep in shape."

She hated that she had something in common with him that was so important to her. Running was the only way she felt even remotely normal.

"How about you?"

"I run, too, to keep in shape." She would die before she admitted that running was her therapy. She didn't care if he was right about her state of mind. First, it was none of his concern. She wouldn't let her pain and guilt get in the way of the investigation and apprehension of the man who was setting fire to La Rosa. Second, she would not give in to her impulses. That's what had gotten her into trouble. She often thought if she hadn't rushed into the house, if she'd taken a bit more time, she might have seen the bomb, the signature of the arsonist she now knew as Vulcan.

But she'd wanted to prove herself. Make the men in the department sit up and take notice. Richard had said she had the gift. Right now she felt as if his words were nothing but ashes of an extinguished fire.

That included the impulse she had to let her eyes linger over Jordan's mouth, the strong lines of his neck, his firm jaw. Getting involved with the man who wanted her off the task force would be akin to suicide. Grace wasn't that crazy.

When their food was delivered, Jordan delved into his sandwich with gusto.

Grace eyed hers and remembered the promise she made to herself. She picked up one of the wedges of her sandwich and dug in.

Jordan wiped his mouth and said, "There have been six more residential fires since you were…injured. Always the same MO."

"The Coke can."

"Yes, and he barricaded the doors as he's always done in the past. This brings up something that has me stumped."

"What?"

"Why did he use a different method with you and your colleagues?"

The investigator in her whipped to attention. "What do you mean?"

He frowned and the movement only made him more appealing. Brooding looked good on Agent Kelly. She thought nothing would look good on him, too.

"I've read the report over and over again looking for an answer, but I still come back to the same question."

With the wedge of her sandwich halfway to her mouth, she asked, "And that is?"

He took a moment to polish off half of his sandwich. "Eat," he said.

To her surprise, Grace brought the sandwich to her mouth and bit into it. The savory flavor of the turkey, ham, cheese, bacon, lettuce and tomato was lost on her. She chewed mechanically and swallowed. She managed to eat the whole thing.

Jordan looked satisfied. He nudged her plate and she picked up a second wedge. "Are you going to force-feed me my meal or your theory?"

He laughed. "My theory is solid, but you look like a stiff wind could blow you over. Eat some more."

"I'll eat. Go on with your theory."

He took a sip of his coffee and nodded. "He used a bomb, not the soda can. It wasn't arson as much as it was a trap."

She set her wedge down as a sick feeling churned in her gut, her food forgotten. "You think he targeted us? For some reason?" This put a more sinister and disturbing twist on the whole situation. Why would the arsonist target all three of them? What could have been the point?

"I can't seem to come up with any other explanation.

Unless, of course, we're dealing with a copycat or a totally different arsonist."

She was sure the man who had blown up her car this morning was the same man who had killed Richard and Sara…for some purpose perhaps? She wasn't totally convinced of that. But for the first time she realized that by joining the task force, by aligning herself with these people, she was putting them directly in danger.

Her heart thundered and it was all she could do to keep it together. Pushing the panic away and compartmentalizing it helped. "It's not a copycat or a different arsonist."

"How can you be sure of that?"

"Just a gut feeling. You'll find out I'm more of an intuitive investigator. I do it all by feel."

"All by feel…" he said. His eyes flared and that damn awareness shivered between them. Trapped by the dark, raw heat, she blushed, felt her cheeks heat. She looked down at her half-eaten sandwich. She had the sudden urge to put on her running shoes.

"Anything else?"

The sharp question by the waitress made her jump, shattered the moment. Grace shook her head.

Jordan's gaze was now on the young girl and Grace breathed a sigh of relief. He said, "Just the check, and thanks."

After she walked away, Jordan said, "So we have some inconsistency here. If this is the same arsonist, and I'm inclined to agree with you, then why did he change his MO for you and your coworkers? I think if we answer that question, we might figure out who this guy is."

She hadn't thought about that at all. Jordan had showed her he was partially right. She and her coworkers had been targeted. But she was still healing. She wasn't going to admit to him he was right about her at all. "That is an angle we should definitely think more about," she said, noncommittal. "He changed his tactics for us. We really need to understand why."

He nodded. "There's also the fact that this guy seems to always be one step ahead of us."

"How so?"

"We had a witness who thought he remembered seeing a car parked outside one of the residential fires, but he couldn't give us the license plate number. He said he would remember, just give him some time. His house was torched the next day and he died in the fire."

Grace couldn't help her reaction any more than she could have stopped breathing. The flashes of memory overtook her, brought her back to the basement, back to the smell of scorched flesh, the sound of crying and her own scream of agony, both physical and mental.

She slid out of the booth abruptly, without an explanation to Jordan. With a deliberateness born of a need for privacy, she headed to the ladies' room. She slammed open the door and went inside. She caught a glimpse of herself in the mirror all wide-eyed and spooked.

With a soft cry of despair, she went into a stall. Sweating profusely, she sat down and rocked back and forth to get control of herself. She did the deep-breathing exercise that always helped. Wishing like hell she had her running shoes, she rode out the panic. When she was sure she could control it, she stuffed it back into that compartment and slammed it shut. At the sink she cleaned up with a cold compress on her flushed cheeks and the back of her neck. Then she took another deep breath and went back to the booth. Sliding inside, she could see that Jordan was concerned, but he said nothing.

"Go on," she prompted, as she deliberately picked up the third wedge of her sandwich and ate it.

Jordan gently touched her arm and she shuddered out a breath.

She wasn't going to admit how much that helped. His persistence drove her crazy, but it was hard to deny that he had a steadying, calming influence. He always seemed to be in control, so certain of himself and his abilities. It wasn't arrogance so much as assuredness. And that was powerful stuff for her right now. It was hard not to be tempted to lean on him. Just for a tiny moment. He was sturdy and strong. The warrior who didn't falter.

She swore silently at her silly, fanciful notions. She'd better get the stars out of her eyes and keep her two feet planted squarely on terra firma.

Complicating that, however, was Jordan, who sat close to her, not touching her but still making it impossible for her to clear her head.

Her awareness of him was as finely tuned as her senses were to the nuances of a fire. Except with him, there was all that sexual energy jacking things up. She cleared her throat, maybe squared her shoulders a little. She picked up the last piece of her lunch and then made the mistake of looking back at him before taking that first bite.

Something about the morning beard shadowing his jaw, the way his hair wasn't quite so naturally perfect, made his eyes darker and enhanced how impossibly thick his eyelashes were. And she really, really needed to stop looking at his mouth. But the ruggedness the stubble lent to his face just emphasized all the more those soft, sculpted lips of his.

"Grace—"

"Go on," she said before he said something they would both regret. She didn't want to acknowledge her breakdown. She didn't want to talk about her momentary weakness. She'd already dealt with it. Put it back where it belonged.

Denial was such a good thing.

He lifted a shoulder, then sat back and released her from that penetrating gaze. "Three days ago he started torching commercial buildings, including one that manufactures self-contained breathing apparatuses. All the buildings except the SCBA one are owned by Jim Lyons."

"Councilman Lyons?"

"Yes, and he's a member of the task force."

"Maybe the arsonist's mocking you."

"Maybe. There may be something to the SCBA angle."

"Why?" she asked. "Because the ones we were wearing that day could have been faulty?"

"I don't know. Just my gut talking."

"Do you often let your gut do the talking?" Grace asked wryly.

"What? Am I one of those new age, sensitive guys? All intuitive?"

The flash of that tantalizing grin threw her for a loop. A no-nonsense woman who usually kept business and pleasure completely separate felt a jump start to her heart. Didn't seem right under these circumstances. She looked away to break the spell. But she couldn't help the smile, or the small laugh.

It was a miracle, as far as she was concerned, that she could actually find humor in anything at this point.

"The circumstances of the explosion call for a deeper and more thoughtful investigation. I'll order up all the information, unless you feel that might be too much for you to handle."

The smile disappeared and Grace straightened. It was a probe and she recognized it as one. It was also a test. One she intended to ace. "It won't be too much for me."

"We'll have to delve into every bit of the evidence we have as well as examine those photos very closely. Are you sure that it won't be too difficult?"

Just to prove to herself that she could, she finished off her sandwich. After wiping her mouth and nudging him to move out of the booth, she said, "This is about much more than my feelings and my ability to maintain my equilibrium under pressure, Jordan. This is about finding a cold-blooded killer. One who stood there and let Sara die. One who would have done the same to me, but I was lucky. Help got to me in time. Sara and Rick never had a chance. I want to see him pay for the murders he has committed, the crimes he has planned and executed."

Jordan slid out of the booth. "Keeping things in perspective is what's important, Grace. That's going to be the challenge."

Grace rose from the booth and brushed past him. She turned to look back at Jordan. "Yes, that is going to be a challenge, and you can scrutinize me all you want and verbally test me, but I won't fail."

Grace walked away, but Jordan's words hit her right

between the shoulder blades. "We'll see, Grace. We'll see."

After a moment's hesitation, she headed for the black SUV parked at the curb.

Okay, he had to admit it to himself. He was pushing too hard. But he knew what happened to a coworker who buckled under the pressure. He didn't want to be too busy or too immersed to miss the signs. It was too important—much too important.

But Grace lived up to her name. She *seemed* as if she was handling the situation with courage and a routine that allowed her to get back to a calm state of mind. It was only this morning that she'd picked up that envelope and had to relive the day she'd almost died.

That, he knew, stuck with a person. He knew that firsthand. He ran his palms down the tops of his thighs, his gut twisting with the memory of cold, lethal steel pressed against his temple.

So why was he being such a jerk?

Damn if he knew.

Grace would look at him with those big baby blues and her wistful gaze, so vulnerable and somehow so strong—it made him go all soft inside. Not something a hard-hitting agent admitted to anyone. Especially not to himself.

Damn Greg Baker for his smarmy, politician way. Bringing Grace onto the task force just wasn't a good decision. But she was determined to stay. Not much he could do to change the situation. No matter how much he wanted to.

He'd have to put his personal biases aside and press on with the investigation. Truth of the matter was, he wasn't going to be easy on Grace. Wouldn't be good for her or for him.

Ah, there was that firsthand knowledge again.

Every one of us lived in our very own personal hells.

You either stood up and took it like a man or you crumbled.

Crumbling wasn't in Jordan Kelly's lexicon.

He'd have to see if it was in Grace Addison's.

Chapter 3

"We should go by your house and pick up what you need. It's best for you to stay at the hotel where I am. We'll get you into an adjoining room."

"Adjoining room?"

He glanced at her and raised an eyebrow.

From the look on her face, he could see that she was fighting an internal battle, one between good sense and independence. She had to get used to the fact that from now on she was a marked woman and she had no choice but to let him act as her bodyguard.

"For your protection, Grace."

"Agent— Jordan, I'm quite capable of making my own decisions. I'm well aware of my situation and that I'm in danger."

"Then that's all the more reason to defer to me. I *was* an FBI agent, remember. I was fully trained in the protection of personnel at the academy."

Grace nodded. It was clear to him that she was finding all this overwhelming.

"Oh, come on. It's a very nice hotel. Palacio de Matador. Absolutely beautiful there."

Jordan watched emotions play across her face through the duskiness of his sunglasses, waiting for her to allow him to proceed. He drew in a deep breath, waging an unspoken battle within himself.

Did she have doubts about putting her life in his hands? The thought tortured him. The images from his lapse in vigilance ghosted in from the past and pointed condemning fingers. He found himself momentarily distracted by their persuasiveness. Wanting to again go over and over the facts, the events, re-creating his failure in his mind, trying to find what he'd missed in Dan that had later caused devastating circumstances.

His self-evaluation never left him alone. It laid down the verdict like a grim hanging judge: he'd failed Dan. He'd failed in his duty as an FBI negotiator. The guilt haunted him. It interrupted his concentration, affected his every waking hour and diminished his sound judgments until finally he was left with only one alternative. He'd had to leave. Some thought he'd left in disgrace, some that he was fired for his inability to realize that Dan was spiraling into instability, traveling down a road that was going to ultimately end in disaster.

He shrugged off those old, unsettling feelings. Pushed away that condemning voice that spoke out of the dark recesses of his mind at every opportunity. They were his private demons and they had their time and place. Now was not the time to indulge them.

"Let's get this over with, then," Grace said. She climbed into the SUV and settled into the seat. Jordan moved behind the wheel, started the car and eased out into traffic. It was heavy for a Monday afternoon. But two blocks over, there was an art fair on the street. Tourists clogged the sidewalks and filled up the eateries along the way. La Rosa was a quaint, beautiful little city. After enduring the bustle and congestion of Los Angeles, it was a welcome assignment.

With Grace's softly murmured directions, he drove out of the city proper and climbed into the foothills that bracketed the city. The road gently curved at a gradual incline, turning back on itself until they were driving on a road that overlooked the city with its sprawling neighborhoods, the clustered high-rises and poured concrete that made up their center of civilization. With a left-hand turn, Jordan followed Grace's directions until she instructed him to turn into an upward-sloping driveway. Once he stopped the car, he took in the surrounding area. She lived on a road that had houses spaced evenly apart, not too close and not too far. Hers was an older stucco home in the Spanish style with heavy wood trim and tile roof. Its spacious front porch was punctuated by many arches.

Grace slipped out of the SUV just as her cell phone rang. She answered it and then looked at him. "My insurance agent," she mouthed as he followed her to the front door. He surveyed the area, but all looked quiet.

He followed her as she led the way, cell phone glued to her ear. She spoke in clipped affirmations of understanding, huddled slightly in distraction. Pulling off his sunglasses, he put a hand on her shoulder as she unlocked the door, signaling that he should enter first. She halted, nodding, continued to talk to the insurance agent while he slipped inside the house. Cautiously, he prowled through every room while she waited in the foyer downstairs. He found himself noting clues about her, the living room with its unfinished painting, and the slight clutter in the kitchen. In her bedroom, the subtle scent of her lingered in the air, a fresh scent that made him want to breathe in deep.

Once he indicated to her that it was safe to enter, she made her way into the living room and sat down on the couch. Pulling a notebook from her bag, she continued to talk to the insurance agent.

When she closed her cell phone, she gave him a wistful smile.

"They're going to get a check to me for a new car in two days," she said. "Since mine was totally demolished, there was no assessing or repairs to talk about."

Jordan hung his sunglasses on his suit pocket.

"It's not lost on me that I could have been in the vehicle at the time of the explosion. It's not the car. It's the violation, the wanton destruction that's so upsetting."

"The sense of being a victim can derail you. That's what he wants." He paused, his mind obviously elsewhere. "Why don't you pack your things and get your house ready to close up. You won't be coming back here until we catch this bastard."

For once she just nodded and headed for the stairs. He noticed the unfinished handrail. It looked as if it had been recently stripped and sanded. Vulcan had disrupted her life.

"While you do that, I'm going to take a look around outside. Before you go up, lock the door behind me."

She stopped and came back. Following him to the door, she waited as he opened it. He paused. "We'll find him, Grace."

"I guarantee it," she said through gritted teeth.

Again with the extreme. Briefly, Jordan considered the underlying current of her vehemence. Weighing whether it was directed at him and then rejecting that assumption. He flashed a grin at her, impressed that she was determined, not fearful.

Perhaps she was remembering how she'd stood in the foyer only this morning with those pictures in her hands, he supposed, reliving that nightmare all over again.

After stepping outside, he waited while she locked the door. He walked around the front of the house looking for anything out of place, but found nothing. Heading around back, he found a wooded area. He paused next to a stand of pine trees and studied the brush and the beds of needles, browned by time, scattered around the base of the trunks.

Someone had been through here recently, judging by the disturbed needles. He saw that some areas were scuffed, exposing the rich black soil beneath. Part of a heelprint was pressed into the earth. The tip of a cigarette butt showed where it had been flipped into a nearby growth of crabgrass. He picked it up and bagged it as evidence. Made a mental note to get the crime scene techs out here to take an imprint of the heel.

He moved behind the trees and placed himself in the same spot, facing the same direction the prowler had.

Angry that someone had stood here and watched Grace's house, he felt a quick rush of emotion that made him seethe. The anger left him gradually, replaced by a brief puzzlement at its intensity.

He looked through the trees, along the same sight line as the person who'd stood there before him. From this spot, he could see her house, including the front and back porches. He had a direct line of sight into her living room and her bedroom windows.

He crouched down slightly, but the boughs of the tree were closer together there, and his sight line was immediately obstructed. A man, then. Or a very tall woman. But his gut told him it was a man.

Women didn't normally conceal their stalking. Men hunted. And the fewer people around to contest the hunt, the better.

Besides, in his experience, women arsonists were rare, but they did make up about 6 percent of the fire-starters. More than half were single males who came from two-parent homes, surprisingly. A great majority of serial arsonists were Caucasian males, setting more than one fire over the course of their lives, with the majority of their fires being set prior to age thirty-five. African-American males set the most one-time arson fires.

So that meant they were probably searching for a twenty- to thirty-five-year-old white male.

He looked over his shoulder and noted the direct path of cover from where he stood, straight through a short stand of woods, to where several other homes were located. After some exploration, he discerned it was only a short hike through another dense stand of trees, then a quick scramble up a rocky slide to where the main road wrapped around the top of the foothill before dipping down the other side toward town.

He didn't want to leave Grace alone for much longer, even in a locked house, but he needed to take the time to track it while he was here.

He looked back at her house in preparation to traverse the slope. As if on cue, she stepped out onto the back porch, a bag of birdseed in her hands. The light caught her hair, and the strands flashed gold in the sun. It fell forward like a cascade of molten sunlight over her delicate shoulder, dazzling him. The light caught the tones of her skin—gave it an engaging glow somehow. She looked almost angelic.

Her slender arms extended, manipulating the opening of the bird feeder to set it on a redwood table and pour the contents of the bag into the container.

He took a deep breath as a bird lighted on the edge of the porch railing, twittering at her as if to say, "It's about time."

Grace's soft laughter traveled to where he was standing, beautiful and melodic.

While he watched her, she crossed the lawn to a shed and pulled out an extension ladder. Placing it against a tree situated close to her house, she climbed. He saw that she had another bird feeder sitting in the branches.

The scrabbling of a squirrel climbing a nearby tree drew his attention. When he looked back, Grace was stowing away the ladder and taking the empty bag back into the house.

He shuttered away any thought of her, just as he'd done in the mayor's office, on the stairs of the town hall and in the diner. He was here to do a job. Grace Addison was a coworker. Rubbing a hand along the back of his neck, he turned away from her house. He began tracing the trail of evidence back through the woods, taking pictures with his slim digital camera.

He serendipitously discovered an empty crushed cigarette pack in the weeds. He snapped a picture of that also, uncertain whether it meant anything. He bagged it, too.

He was doing whatever it took to keep his thoughts focused exclusively on the situation here. Trying like hell not to get wound up about the woman he was working with.

He moved swiftly through the trees and up the side of the rise until he came out to the road. He paused for a moment to catch his breath and enjoy the gorgeous view of the town below.

He hadn't expected to feel peace here, not sure he was entitled to it. He hadn't expected to enjoy this town as much as he did. He snapped a few more shots. With one last look at the city he'd sworn to protect, he headed back to Grace's house.

His steps were fast and curt, his impatience lined his body. What he really wanted to do was dig a little more, find out who the hell was watching her, threatening her, track that bastard down and make the whole problem go away.

When he knocked on the door and heard her ask who it was, he applauded her caution.

"Jordan," he responded.

She immediately opened the door. He noticed that she'd changed into a pair of black yoga pants and a pink T-shirt that did nice things to her skin. Simple, demure clothing, yet his pulse kicked up a notch and his body tightened in immediate response.

Her mouth was pinched at the corners. Clearly she was annoyed about this whole bodyguard thing. Perversely, that made him want to smile.

She said, "What were you doing out there?"

He debated whether or not to talk to her about the fact that she had been watched—and often, judging by the disturbance he'd witnessed.

Figuring he'd have to tell her sooner or later, he opted for blunt honesty. "I was doing a perimeter check."

"A perimeter check?" she asked with a raised eyebrow. "Does this include a full special ops team?"

"Nope, don't need one. I'm a one-man juggernaut,"

he responded, giving in to the grin that threatened out of nowhere. She frustrated him to the extreme in ways he didn't begin to try and understand. She sure as hell couldn't know. He should have stayed in LA, gone into firearms control and chased scumbag gun traffickers. Getting shot at or blown up was preferable to dealing with this inner turmoil.

"Grace—"

"Let me guess. My friend doesn't just like leaving me mail. He likes to watch me?" She shifted away from the door so he could enter. Closing it and locking it, she clenched her hands into fists at her side.

"Yes."

She tensed further, and he could see her wage her own internal battle. He searched her face and her eyes for any telltale sign of a breakdown.

"It's a good thing I have blinds."

"There's more," he told her, deciding there was no point in sugarcoating anything. He wanted to drive home the importance of staying close to him, and laying it out as bluntly as possible was probably best. He could only hope she would quit the task force so the job of guarding her could fall to someone else.

Her slender throat worked. Without a word he could tell that she was rallying her internal barriers.

"Out with it, then."

"He's been watching you for some time, Grace. Perhaps weeks, maybe months."

She simply stared at him and, for a second, dropped her guard. She looked tired, and he wondered if she had the same kind of nightmares that he had. He stopped that train of thought. Not good to have anything in common with her. He didn't know what was going on inside her pretty head. All he wanted to do was make sure she didn't lose it.

"Stop staring at me like I'm going to dissolve in front of you," she snapped.

He shrugged. "I don't think you're—"

"Like hell you don't. I'm a full partner in this whole thing. It's true that I've been targeted and I've just come off medical leave, but I'm *not* fragile!"

"I'll reserve my judgment on that, Grace."

She went past him toward her bags, indicating that she considered the conversation over. "You go to hell, Jordan."

He shot her a sideways glance. There was deep anger there, not just irritation. Most people reacted that way when faced with the truth. Did she think she was fragile? What was she concealing from him? She had to know he would discover it sooner or later.

"Do you want to tell me why you're really so angry?"

"It's none of your business." She glanced at him, and then shifted her gaze firmly back to her bags. When he tried to help her, she slapped his hands away and picked them up herself. "We're not friends. I'm well aware of that, so I'm not going to paint my nails with you and share all my innermost secrets."

Her quick retreat behind cool blue eyes triggered something in him. Some reckless thing he couldn't control. He found himself grinning in the face of her aloof anger, as cocky as he'd ever been and completely unrepentant. "I'm partial to passion-red," he said.

She dropped her bags, and they made a thud as they hit the wooden floor. "That is absolutely the worse color for you," she said. "You should stick with the pinks."

To her credit, a hint of a smile briefly curved her lips, but the light didn't reach as far as her eyes.

The woman was quick-witted. Something else he liked about her. He had the urge to touch her. Certainly not the first time and probably wouldn't be the last time. But he refrained. The hand-slapping was fresh in his mind. There was no guessing what she would slap or put a knee into if he reached out for her.

"I won't pretend to know who you are, but I do know you're in trouble. That's where I come in."

She bristled. "I don't want anyone's help."

"But the fact still remains that you need help. And I'm here. We're joined at the hip. You'd be a fool if you were blind to the situation."

She let out a short laugh at that. "You'd be surprised. I'm not feeling all that smart here lately." She looked at him, studying his face, as if trying to find something there to help her understand. "Too bad we didn't meet under normal circumstances."

"Are you saying we might have actually been friends?" he said with a mock gasp.

She shot him a look, and he couldn't tell if she was amused or annoyed. Probably a little of both. Something he was thinking they'd both likely have to get used to if they were going to be spending any serious time together.

"Maybe."

He couldn't help but see the faint shadows beneath her eyes, the strain tightening the skin at the corners of her mouth. She wasn't smiling, but something had softened in her voice all the same. His own smile came more naturally now. "You say that like it's a bad thing. I'm a good guy to have in your corner."

"I'll reserve my judgment on that, Jordan."

His recently uttered words were not lost on him. "Fair enough, Grace."

"Fair? Hmm. Nothing's fair in my book. Nothing at all."

She picked up a bag and shoved it into his chest, and his air escaped with a soft oof. That seemed to give her pleasure. She went to pick up the next bag, but then straightened. "On second thought, since you're the strong, virile male, why don't you carry all my bags?" With that she snagged her purse, turning toward the door. When she opened it, she looked back at him. "Come on, man, put your back into it." Without another word she went out the door.

The first part of the ride back into town was quiet. He'd stowed her bags in the backseat, repressing a strong, rascally urge to exit the house empty-handed. When they drove away from her house, he noticed how she looked back. He wasn't sure whether it was regret for being away or relief that she would no longer be exposed to Vulcan's scrutiny.

He broke the silence. "Do you own a sidearm?"

"Yes. And I know how to use it."

"You do?"

"I was training to become an arson investigator, Jordan. It's required. You know, to catch the bad guys and to protect myself." She rolled her eyes.

He made a show of sighing at her. "That's very valley girl," he said.

"What is?"

"Rolling your eyes. Did you grow up in the valley?"

She snorted. "Like, no."

He laughed. "Okay, just asking."

He braked for a stop sign, glancing to make sure the way was clear before proceeding.

"Do you have the weapon with you?" he asked finally.

"Yes, it's in my bag."

He cast her a glance. "How much have you used the gun?"

"I took the police training course. I've used the weapon for target practice, but that was limited."

"Okay, so maybe we should think about getting you on the range. Getting trained will give you an edge if you come up against the guy and for some reason you're alone."

"It's realistic to think you can't be with me 24/7."

"I intend to be as close to you as I can get."

The sudden silence was heavy with tension. Grace looked over at him, but he kept his eyes on the road. His body reacted to his words, though. His pulse sped, his body tingled. Just the thought of Grace's soft skin beneath his hands made him want to pull the SUV over and indulge himself.

When she faced forward, he hazarded a glance at her. The telltale stain on her cheeks made his blood pressure zing. She was blushing, which meant she was thinking about what it would be like to be close to him. He wasn't sure how he felt about that. The temptation was easier to resist when he wasn't confident how Grace would feel about him touching her.

Or, it could be that it didn't bother him as much as he wanted it to, and that, maybe, he even liked it. Getting involved with Grace in her state of mind and while they were working together was tantamount to kicking his career into the gutter and watching it slide into oblivion. Not smart.

He would keep his hands off her, he promised himself. Even if it killed him.

He glanced at her; his gaze snagged on those legs stretched out over the black leather seat, how her yoga pants molded over those long legs of hers…and he remembered why he hated playing by the rules. He watched her adjust her seat belt with a delicate pink-tipped hand. Sighing, he resigned himself to the fact that most of his showers in the near future were likely to be long and very, very cold.

They pulled into town just then, and his thoughts were mercifully dragged away from Grace.

Palacio de Matador was a quaint, two-story classical Spanish-style hotel with tile-roofed porticos and easy access to the beach. A huge mural of a matador, in the style of Diego Rivera, waving an enormous cape at a charging bull, was emblazoned on the side of the hotel. Two figures created much larger than life—their battle grand and out of proportion.

He parked in the back of the hotel and said, "Let's get you checked in."

She nodded and followed him out of the vehicle and into the cool confines of the enormous hotel lobby. The floor was tiled in cold blue stone and a sign set into a three-legged stand declared a promise of lobster-stuffed salmon for dinner. At the lobby's far end a young clerk stood attired in a black tuxedo behind a golden desktop.

At the desk, Jordan said, "Miss Addison will need a room, one that is adjoining to mine. Is that possible?"

The young clerk pulled up something on the computer and searched it for a moment. "Yes, sir," he said. "There is an adjacent room that is right next door to yours and it is currently vacant. How long will you be staying with us, Miss Addison?"

"I'm not sure."

He nodded, shrugging, "That's no problem. We will leave it open-ended then?"

"Yes, for now."

"Fill out this form for your room, please," the clerk said, handing her a small card and pen. "How will you pay?"

"My Visa card," Grace said.

"May I process that now?"

Grace dug into her purse, handed him her credit card and went back to writing.

He processed her registration and her payment, handing her the keycard.

"Go ahead to the room," Jordan said. "I'll get the bags." He then turned on his heel and strode across the lobby toward the double glass doors.

"Where is this room?" she asked the clerk.

The clerk pointed to a set of elevators directly across the room from his desk.

"When you get to the second floor, turn left and follow the hall to room 262."

After a few moments, Jordan stood in front of the door and knocked. She opened it and he entered with her bags, depositing them near the bed.

"I think it would be a good idea to get in some range practice," Jordan said.

"Today?"

"Do you have something else you need to do?"

"I thought we could get started on the case."

Jordan shrugged. "I think it's best to assess your skills with a weapon."

Without a word, Grace strode up to him. She pushed

aside his suit jacket and reached inside, the brush of her hand against his lower chest like a lick of flame. She curled her hand around the butt of his gun and pulled it from the holster. She sat down on the bed and with precision and ease disassembled the gun.

She smiled slightly and just as easily put the gun back together and, after setting the safety, smugly offered it to him, butt first.

He made no attempt to take the gun back. Something inside of him wanted to see what she would do. He wanted her to put the gun back into his holster. Hell, he wanted more than that, and he knew it. "I believe people should put things back where they found them."

Her eyes widened, then narrowed. She shifted off the bed and walked up to him, looking up at him in that intent, open way she sometimes did. He could imagine others found it a tad unnerving, that sort of overt directness. And that she'd intended it to be. For him it was more unsettling than unnerving. It would serve her well in interrogation.

She ran her hand down the lapel of his suit coat, using her wrist to flick it aside. He endured the brush of her fingertips. With deliberate slowness, she slid the gun into the worn leather, inch by inch. The back of her hand brushed along his chest wall. Pinpricks of pleasure, left in the wake of her touch, traveled along his skin to settle in his groin.

"There you go," she said softly. "All safe and sound."

He let out a breath and turned away. "I'm going to change out of this suit. We're going to the range. Your little show doesn't change the fact that I haven't seen you hit anything with a bullet."

"I can think of a good target right now."

He turned and threw her a rakish grin as he pulled open the door and made his escape.

Grace might have been through a lot in the last few months, but the woman knew how to stand up for herself. She'd risen to his bait, and he needed a moment away from her to gather his composure. He could see how she had made it this far in her career.

It wasn't easy for a woman to become a firefighter, even in the twenty-first century. The old prejudices still lingered among the good ole boys and the new up-and-coming recruits who simply didn't want the competition. So he admired her—hell, too damn much. He had to keep his perspective.

But was the backbone she had shown hiding something? Was she a time bomb ticking away? He'd missed it before, and that had led to a terrible, tragic loss. He couldn't go back and make it right. He couldn't save Dan or anyone else who had died that day. But he could make sure Grace didn't lose it and compromise the task force and its mission.

Grace let out a breath as the door closed behind Jordan. She sat down heavily on the bed, trying to still her racing heart. Her hand still tingled where it had come into contact with his chest. Okay, so she was just trying to show off. The man made her so damn mad.

He didn't think she was capable. In fact, he thought she was going to lose it any minute. Well, she was determined to prove him wrong.

She thought she was ready when he knocked on the door, but when she opened it she had to catch her breath. Jordan was dressed in a tight black T-shirt with the ATF logo embossed on the right-hand side, his biceps bulging just below the hem of the short sleeves. His hair was mussed and he had a hint of beard stubble lightly shadowing his jaw. But the coup de grâce was the sinfully tight jeans that showed off the heavy, thick muscles in his thighs.

Somehow her life had turned into an action-adventure flick when she wasn't looking. And the leading man was Jordan Kelly.

"You ready to show me some more tricks, Calamity Jane?"

"I think the last one got me into some hot water."

His grin was slow, confident and downright devastating to her already engaged libido. What was she thinking, taunting him like that? It couldn't go very far. She wouldn't let it. She self-consciously rubbed at the back of her neck. She had the almost overwhelming urge to run.

He led the way out of the hotel. She used the time to get her thoughts in order. Not to mention getting her physical reaction to him under control.

But just when she thought she had it beat, he opened the door for her. After closing it, he braced his arms on the windowsill. The movement bunched up those arms, delineating the heavy muscle, and he said, "Don't look so worried. I'm sure you'll be able to hit some of the targets."

"Those are fighting words, Kelly."

"Good," he said with a cocky grin.

He walked around to the driver's side. When he slid into the SUV, she secretly watched the play of muscles along his thigh and forearm as he shifted gears and floored the gas when he hit the road.

This was bad. She was hot for her partner.

Chapter 4

Grace adjusted the safety goggles and the ear protectors and reached for the department issued Glock .40. The molded, high-impact nylon stock fit smoothly into her slick palm. Her thumb slid into the curved rest. She picked up the clip.

The feel of the gun in her hand triggered the memory of that day and suddenly her hand started to sweat.

They had been at the range for target practice. She and Richard. It was part of her training and he never skimped, ever. He was a methodical man, but he always did everything with a sense of humor and utter competence.

That day was no different. She wasn't sure if it was tears or sweat that suddenly made her eyes sting now.

They had just finished the session when they'd gotten the call. A botched attempt at arson. Richard had told Grace she could tag along. It would be an excellent chance for her to flex her arson-investigator muscles. Richard said, jokingly, he wouldn't be around much longer.

The words chilled her to the bone.

He was due to retire. Only days away from a fishing boat in the Keys and long, lazy days that had been earned through thirty years of service. But that fishing boat remained empty.

She had been excited, eager to prove herself. Make him proud.

She'd gone over and over that day in her mind so many times, looking for where she'd gone wrong. Where she'd made the mistake that had set off the chain reaction that had killed people she cherished. Two human lives forever lost, lying heavily on her conscience.

Now she knew the truth. Now she knew that it was a trap.

Planned.

The arsonist was taking out the competition. The very people who could bring him to justice. It made Grace wonder how close Richard had gotten to discovering who he was.

"Grace? You okay?"

"I'm fine. I'm fine," she replied, the lie hanging heavy on her tongue. "Don't rush me."

"No need to rush. Just fire when you're ready."

Concentrating, she closed out the noise around her. Extending her arms, she pulled the hammer back with her thumb. In that quiet place, she fired. Pulled the trigger again and fired. The knowledge that the arsonist had so callously stood at the other end of that camera in a safe and comfortable place and watched Sara die made the image of the silhouette blur and change to be replaced by the faceless killer. She pulled the trigger faster, homed in on each impact of the bullet as it hit. Over and over again, she fired, until the sound of the trigger clicking uselessly on the empty pistol registered. But she couldn't stop.

Jordan was there, behind her, his big hand wedging between her finger and the gun, gently manipulating until she released the trigger.

"I want him dead just as much as you do."

His large hand dwarfed hers as he took the gun she released and placed it alongside the two loaded magazines.

He stood next to her, but she hadn't realized he'd raised his gun until he started shooting. Shots rang out in quick succession and his hand never wavered once in his firm grip. On the last shot, the slide locked open on the empty gun.

His arm stayed around her for a long moment, as if he was commiserating with her, regret weighing heavy on him. He stepped back, but she didn't turn around. She picked up her own gun and slid the clip out, the slide forward, and released the hammer to the Safe position.

He pulled in the target and studied the cluster of shots.

Hers were a bit more evenly spaced apart, while his formed a nice tight pattern. She could venture a guess that he was a better shot than Richard, even though it seemed he'd barely taken aim. He'd been fast, exceptionally accurate.

"Not bad, Grace. With a little more practice you could be really good."

"As an arson investigator, I don't expect I'll have to fire a weapon that often."

At that she looked up at him. She'd expected derision,

mockery, scorn, something other than compassion in his blue, blue eyes.

Grace knew it wasn't the right emotion, this anger that seemed to come from some unending well of rage. She clenched her teeth.

She was trying to hold everything together, but it just seemed to be unraveling as fast as she could contain it. And in that moment she hated Jordan Kelly for knowing her weakness, hated him with a fierce passion for the understanding and compassion in his stirring blue eyes.

Unnerved by her reaction, she watched as Jordan grabbed another sheet and reeled it back out. He picked up her gun and handed it to her. Her fingers closed around the grip. With deliberate concentration, she aimed down the sight.

She had to remain calm and guarded. She couldn't let Jordan's intense gaze on her back distract her. She would have to ignore the way her skin prickled all over as he watched, judged. All those questions she'd effectively dodged, yet he would know that, no matter how she'd lied, she was still trapped in that dark, smoky basement.

She could almost feel the burn of that fire. She inhaled a sharp breath at the remembered pain.

Letting everything go until she was empty inside, she aimed at the target and thumbed back the hammer. Depressing the trigger, her shots cracked out, muted by her ear protectors. The bullets slammed into the target, the paper jumping. No matter what, she wouldn't stop. If she let her emotions get the better of her, her anxiety overcome her, she'd never get past her fear. She'd forever be trapped in this waking nightmare. Even with Jordan behind her, reaching his own conclusions, she couldn't back down.

Not if she wanted to be an arson investigator.

And she did. She wanted her life back the way it had been. She wanted to be comfortable in her own skin again, not feeling this sense of dislocation that left her uneasy all the time, a stranger to herself. Damn Jordan Kelly.

The silhouette fluttered in an errant breeze, seemed to mock her.

How would she handle it when they finally tracked him down? Would he resist? Would he force them to use the gun she held, heavy in her hand? Would that put an end to her guilt and fear?

Is that what she needed? she thought. His death? At her hands? Is that what it would take to release her?

She had no answers. She just kept firing, emptying the chamber. She lowered the gun, feeling as empty and spent as the shell casings that littered the floor.

"I need a run."

"Okay, change and I'll meet you in five minutes."

She wanted to scream, *Alone!* She wanted to run *alone.* "Look, Jordan, I don't really need you to tag along. I don't think Vulcan can make me spontaneously combust."

He turned to look at her and she wanted to dissolve into invisibility to escape that look. With the memory of her uncharacteristic behavior at the shooting range, she couldn't handle his keen scrutiny.

In two strides he was close to her. "No, he can't make you spontaneously combust, but he could overpower you and kidnap you. Tie you up and set fire to whatever structure he wants to use as your funeral pyre. You're not going anywhere without me."

She knew he was right. She just hated the reminder and the fact that, until Vulcan was apprehended, Jordan would be her constant companion.

As the door closed behind him, she made a face at him and stuck out her tongue. Not mature, but since he didn't see her, she could indulge herself in juvenile behavior and relieve some of her frustration.

She dressed in angry, jerky movements, muttering under her breath about pushy agents and stupid, he-man attitudes. But, in the end, she stepped outside her door and waited for him.

This time she didn't have to imagine what Jordan's thighs looked like. When he stepped out of his room in a pair of gray athletic shorts, she got the full, hard, lean view of him. His worn T-shirt came to the edge of his rib cage, the frayed ends showing off a set of six-pack abs.

Even though she hadn't taken a step, she found it quite difficult to breathe.

Dammit.

With a self-conscious twist of her shoulder, she was all too aware of the perfection of his body and hers in contrast. Smooth skin was a thing of the past.

He tucked his keycard in his sock just as she had done, and together they headed for the lobby.

Outside, Grace didn't hesitate to take off. She accelerated into a fast lope, soon leaving the hotel behind and dropping into the wooded trail specifically designed for quick access to the marsh and beach beyond.

A nature center was nearby, a popular tourist attraction. Grace increased her speed, needing to shed the vulnerability, the sense of loss, the failure, all wrapping around her and making her muscles tight.

As she moved, the rhythm of her muscles, the even breathing, the wide-open spaces helped some. It would have been perfect if Jordan hadn't been dogging her every step. The presence of him felt too intimate, as if he shared in her pain and the cathartic act of running to purge it for an hour.

They ran through the marsh, swiftly making their way along a gravel trail partly covered by wooden walkways. As they trotted over a curved wooden bridge, ducks paddled within the large shimmering pond to their left and a bittern, thinking it was spotted, stood with its bill pointed upward, blending into the cattails and reeds. A white crane perched on the bank of the small pool, its long legs hidden in the bracken, called out to its mate swimming among the lilies.

Marsh gave way to beachfront. The sand beneath her feet shifted each time her sneaker hit for her stride forward. It felt too much like her life.

She heard a rumble in the distance and looked up at the sky. It was darkening, a storm coming in fast from the sea. She cursed under her breath and knew she should turn back, but decided to go just a bit farther.

Without warning, lightning flashed, making her heart jump. Thunder boomed and it went through flesh and bone like the hard rhythm of a bass drum.

She could smell the ozone in the air, and the faint scent of burning. She stopped abruptly, her blood rushing.

"We should head back," Jordan yelled over the crash of thunder and the jagged blaze of light.

She nodded, the burning air setting off an uncontrollable panic inside her. She turned around and ran back the way they had come, her strides longer, her breathing labored.

When they hit the beginning of the trail back to the hotel, the sky opened up and a deluge poured down on them. They took cover beneath a stand of trees, the downpour minimized by the thick leaves branching out above them.

Thunder crashed with a great booming explosion. The sound jolted her insides. Jordan leaned over her in an attempt to shelter her from the rain. Grace turned her head and their eyes met, fused like heated glass.

As her stomach tumbled over and over in quick succession, everything seemed to slow down, even the rain. Jordan's eyes flashed, the warmth of his body surrounding her both a haven and a boon. His head lowered and her heart pounded, her mouth aching to feel his lips. *Just once, just a taste,* she thought. He was whisper-close, his mouth almost touching hers, when a bolt of lightning flashed, sizzling the air. Jordan jerked away and said, "We'd better find safer cover."

Grace nodded, not sure if she was relieved or disappointed.

With a cry at the cold water hitting her heated skin, Grace followed Jordan from their makeshift shelter. She slipped a bit, but Jordan turned in time and caught her before she fell.

They hit the lobby doors without slowing and ducked inside, the air-conditioning instantly frigid on her wet skin.

She was shivering when she got to her room. She dug her keycard out of her sock and opened the door. Grace didn't need any encouragement to step inside.

"You need to get out of those wet things and into a hot shower."

"Thank you, Mother Jordan. I think I can handle it."

"Okay," he said. "I'll be back in a few so that we can get dinner."

"I'll just eat in my room and turn in. I'm very tired."

Jordan turned to look at her and nodded. "All right. Let's leave your door to my room open. I'll crack mine. Knock if you need me."

"I will."

She had no intention of knocking on his door for anything. He stood with his hand on the doorknob, his eyes shrewd. He pulled off the wet half shirt and wiped his dripping face, his muscles flexing. She couldn't look away from him. She wanted to. She wanted to just turn and walk away, as if that was as easy as she wished it to be.

Her gaze dropped to his sleek, muscled chest gleaming in the light, to his broad, well-defined shoulders and heavy biceps, then stalled on his masculine mouth. Quivers rose in her belly, shimmered over her nerves.

His eyes held hers. And for several heartbeats neither spoke. Lightning flickered on the smooth walls. A door closed next door. And an understanding curled between them, a connection.

And something more.

Something far more primal.

"Grace…" he said, his voice a husky rasp.

"Good night, Jordan," she said, finding the willpower to turn away. She retreated into the dim interior of the bathroom as the connecting door closed.

She couldn't forget that Jordan Kelly had his own agenda. Getting involved with him would be a monumental mistake. She had more to worry about then getting mixed up with a man who thought she was unstable, didn't trust her and wanted her off the task force. A man stalked her. Wanted her dead. That's what she needed to focus on.

Her hands trembled. Thunder rattled through the night sky like an ominous warning, making the nerves along her belly churn.

She forced her thoughts from her stalker, the fear, and concentrated on getting her wet clothes off and herself under the water as it heated up. But even as she slipped under the spray, she couldn't shake the longing she felt to take comfort from Jordan's courage, his nearness, his strength.

She wanted her life back, and it was going to be a battle against a relentless and merciless foe.

That was what she needed to save her energy to face.

She couldn't breathe.

Fire was all around her, searing her skin, her lungs. She turned her head and reached out for Sara, needing to be a comfort for the dying woman, not thinking about her own life as it slipped away.

But when she turned her head, when she looked, it wasn't Sara's eyes staring back at her. Jordan lay next to her, his blue eyes filled with regret, pain and guilt. He reached out to her as if she was the only person in the world who could give him relief, absolution. She tried to move her hand, tried to force her arm to extend, but she couldn't. She was paralyzed, and she watched as Jordan's eyes filled with immeasurable pain as the life seeped out of him.

She woke with a cry, her whole body trembling. The sounds of the storm receding.

And he was there. In the darkness he touched her

and that was all it took. She remembered the dream, the utter sense of loss and desolation she felt. She wrapped her arms around his neck and held on to him, not fully awake, nightmares chasing her.

He cupped the back of her head, his palm lightly caressing, his fingers moving deeper between the strands.

His seductive scent filled her and she breathed deep—so masculine.

When he traced his thumb down her neck, letting it rest in the hollow of her throat, she felt the rough caress in a rippling shiver running all the way down to her bare toes.

"You okay?" he said eventually, his voice low, his thumb moving in a slow circle around her throat.

"Yes," she whispered. "Damn nightmares."

Jordan nodded grimly. "Damn nightmares," he echoed, as if he knew exactly what she was talking about. It quirked her interest, but she didn't voice her thoughts. "I heard you call out. Want to talk about it? That might help."

"It's just a jumble," she lied.

"All those fears and regrets assail us in the dark, huh?"

"I guess so," she agreed. She never used to be afraid of the dark.

She felt him retreat and the light snapped on. He studied her face. "Think you can sleep now?"

She instantly missed feeling his arms around her, but pushed that away. She was being such a fool.

She nodded. "I'll be fine."

He turned off the light, and Grace lay back down, trying to forget his warmth and his comfort. They were fleeting anyway.

* * *

Jordan used all his frustration to bang on the ornate wooden door in front of him.

When Greg Baker answered, looking disheveled and alarmed, Jordan pushed his way past him into the house. Greg's wife was standing in the hallway, her eyes also concerned. When she saw Jordan, she gave her husband a firm glance and said, "I'm heading upstairs to bed, Greg. Make sure the doors are locked."

Greg nodded and smiled at his wife as she went up the stairs.

"My study," he said, running his hands over his hair in a vain attempt to smooth it.

Jordan followed, the irrational anger he felt permeating his every step. As soon as the door closed behind them, Greg said, "Problem?"

"Yes, you son of a bitch. There's a problem. I want Grace off the task force. Assign someone to protect her, but get her out of this."

"No can do. She's an important part—"

"There is no audience here, Greg," Jordan said, low and soft. "Just you and me. I know why she's on the task force. It doesn't have anything to do with her being an integral part of the team and we both know it. You're just covering your ass and getting some good publicity out of it."

Greg sighed, moving away. He gave his eye a rub and sat down in his desk chair, looking tired. "Listen, Jordan, I don't know where you came up with something like that. The pressures of this office and how I deal with them are not your concern. I brought you down from LA to give me a hand. If you want me to call your superior…"

Jordan leaned toward him angrily, placing both hands on his desk.

"Do you think I give a damn about that? This is a woman who has been through enough. She can't handle this."

"Is it her or is it you?" Greg asked, his eyebrows elevated, his eyes piercing. "We both know that what happened with the FBI hasn't been easy for you."

"I'm going to forget we're friends, Greg, if you continue with that train of thought." Jordan straightened, ran his hands through his hair and rubbed the back of his neck.

Greg rocked back in his chair, grimacing, giving Jordan's threat an impatient wave of dismissal. "Don't give me that juvenile 'We ain't gonna be friends anymore' crap, Jordan. Doesn't work on me. I think maybe you're projecting here, don't you?"

"Projecting?"

"It was tragic what happened to Dan Matthews. But you were a negotiator, not his shrink. You need to let it go," Greg said. He picked up a bottle of aspirin from the desk and opened it.

Jordan scoffed silently.

Greg swallowed a pill, casting Jordan a glare as he did so.

"Don't sit there denying it. You wear it on you like a goddamn kick-me sign and try to say it's not there. Only what's written on it is all about how Agent Jordan single-handedly let down the whole Federal Bureau of Investigation. As if there is a mandate for extra-sensory perception in you as part of your worth or something."

"I should have seen it coming."

Greg shook his head and huffed. "You think you

could have prevented him from doing what he did? No one can see into another person's mind, Jordan. It's not possible."

Greg rose from his chair, clapped Jordan on the shoulder and propelled him out of his study and into the hall. "What I need you to do is get your head into this investigation and get me some results. Grace might surprise you. She has an impeccable record."

Jordan came to a full stop and said, "She's just barely hanging on emotionally."

Greg shrugged. "Regardless, I need her on the task force and what I say goes. Work that out or pack up and go back to LA. And I'll get someone who can."

Jordan could see that the conversation was over. He turned to leave.

"Oh, and, Jordan…"

Jordan turned back.

"…try to find a more reasonable hour to visit," Greg continued, casting him a wink and nod. "The wife, she gives me an earful about working late, and when my work follows me home she hits the roof."

Jordan went out Greg's front door, knowing that talking to Greg wasn't going to do any good. He could try reasoning with Grace again, but it was clear to him that she considered what she was doing imperative. Probably thought she needed it for her own peace of mind. It was up to him to keep a close eye on her and try to assess her stability.

Unless he could get her to quit outright. Wouldn't that just suit him? He knew what it meant to be a liability. He'd lost his job at the FBI because he simply couldn't perform it. But, Grace… Jordan shook his head as he started the car. Grace didn't give up. He surely had to give her credit for that. As he drove back to the hotel, he had to wonder if Greg wasn't right. Was he the one who couldn't handle it?

Grace woke with a start. She saw Jordan's light on under the door and she walked over to it and opened it a crack. "Jordan?"

She heard the rustle of cloth as a man rose, the squeak of leather.

"No, Grace. It's me."

Grace froze for a minute at the voice of Sara's husband. What was he doing here?

"Tom?"

"Yes, Detective Russo assigned me this duty. He got a call from Agent Kelly."

Her mouth twisted. Figured that chauvinistic cop would send Tom Parker over here. "Where did Agent Kelly go?"

She opened the door wider so she could see his face. Tom hadn't changed much. He still had the same red hair, the same pockmarked hatchet face and the same piercing blue eyes.

He stood in front of the chair he'd been sitting in. A couple of soda cans, a tiny empty bottle of hot sauce and a newly opened pack of cigarettes lay on the table near him, one cigarette missing from it. This was new to Grace. Tom never smoked. One of the soda cans had ashes on its rim.

"He had to see the mayor. Said it was urgent. How have you been, Grace?"

"Recovering and trying to stay busy."

"You made it to Sara's funeral."

"I had to go, Tom. She was my best friend." Emotion edged her words.

"I wasn't in my best form that day. I'd just lost Sara and I...blamed you a little bit because you were here and she wasn't."

"Of course. I understand." Nervous tension tightened her stomach. "How have you been, Tom?"

"I'm fine. I go to work, go home and cook for myself." Grace sensed a tension about him, humming like electricity in the air. His eyes were hooded, his face tight. "But I guess you're familiar with that, aren't you? Being single and all."

For a moment Tom was silent. Grace found his eyes locked on hers. Tom said nothing, but the look in his eyes was flinty. Hardened. A pair of azure agates.

Just then Jordan came through the door. Tom's hand went to his gun until he realized who it was.

"Thanks for coming, Officer Parker."

"No problem, sir. Let me know if you need me again." Tom paused to tuck the cigarette pack into a shirt pocket, "Goodbye, Grace."

When the door closed behind Tom, Grace came fully into Jordan's room. "Tom Parker, Jordan?"

"Yes, seems Detective Russo thinks that was a good idea. I didn't want to send for another officer since it was already getting late. I figured you wouldn't even know he was here. I had to—"

"Talk to the mayor. What was so important it couldn't wait until morning?"

"I told him he should remove you from the task force."

"You what?"

"Grace, this is too personal for you and is putting a strain on you. You haven't fully recovered from your trauma, neither physically nor mentally. I think that you should recognize your limitations and let me get you someplace safe."

"My limitations? You're worried that I'll snap. You think I can't be trusted to handle the stress. You have no right to go to the mayor and try to get me removed. You haven't even given me a chance."

Jordan stalked to the window and leaned against the casement. He breathed deeply, as if trying to get his composure. "I'm...concerned about you. I...don't want you to be hurt. You've been through enough. Although I admire your courage..."

"You don't trust me."

"No, I don't."

"Then I guess it will be up to me to prove to you that I'm trustworthy."

She slammed the door as she exited. It echoed as she slipped back into bed and turned out the light.

She would make sure she proved Jordan Kelly wrong. Her very life depended on it.

Chapter 5

Grace dressed very carefully for her first day at the task force. A black skirt, pink button-down shirt and matching black jacket. She wanted to look professional and in command. The nightmare last night flashed through her mind. His dead eyes haunted her.

That was just a nightmare. It was only her subconscious taking over. She didn't have to give it any credence.

And she wouldn't.

When she met Jordan, he was impeccably dressed, as usual.

They went to the restaurant in the hotel where Grace ate sparingly, her stomach knotted with tension from yesterday. She would have to prove herself to Jordan and it rankled. Truthfully, she only had to work with him. Nothing else. So why did it matter so much to her what he thought?

She remembered her conversation with Tom last night, his unnerving behavior. This brought her thoughts back to Sara and how she had wanted to talk to Grace. Grace hadn't been able to see her friend before the explosion and her subsequent death. For the first time she wondered if it had something to do with her husband Tom.

She was probably seeing things in Tom that weren't there. Her guilt did strange things to her.

She let it go. She had enough to deal with today— meeting the task force members, digging through the open cases that involved Vulcan and reliving her nightmare in pictures all over again.

"Are you ready to go?" Jordan asked.

Grace nodded, wiping the corners of her mouth with a napkin. "How many people are on the task force?" she inquired, standing up.

"Six, including us," Jordan replied, taking her elbow and moving toward the exit. "But make no mistake. The councilman is there for show. He hasn't been much help. The ADA is sharp. You already know Detective Russo and your fire chief, Mike Lawrence."

Grace strode with him, pausing momentarily as he held open the glass doors of the restaurant for her. "Mike's on the team? He's very knowledgeable."

Jordan nodded, entering the hotel lobby after her. "He is and he's been good at pointing out similarities in the fires so we can classify the ones that are related to Vulcan."

"That's helpful, but it might be smart for us to go back and research fires that could have been set by Vulcan. We might get something out of that. At least a pattern."

"That's a good idea, Grace. We'll have to get started

on that. We don't lack for equipment. The mayor has provided us with top-notch stuff."

"Ooh, toys. What fun."

They made their way across the lobby of the hotel and were almost to the doors when the desk clerk called out, "Miss Addison."

Grace turned and walked to the desk. "Yes?"

The clerk reached under the desk. Another clerk, a woman with very dark hair was typing on the computer. "A package was dropped off for you."

Grace looked down at what the clerk was holding and backed up a step. It was another nine-by-twelve plain brown envelope. She took a deep breath. "Jordan…" she said, her words trailing off.

"What's wrong?" When he saw the envelope, he said, "Set it down on the counter."

The clerk at the computer gave Jordan a startled look. The male one complied, then both of them moved away like it was a live bomb.

"We should get this dusted for prints first," Grace said, her throat constricted.

Jordan pulled out two evidence bags from his suit coat pocket. Using one as a protective glove to pick up the envelope, he gingerly dropped it inside the second bag.

"Who left this for me?" Grace asked the clerk.

"I'm sorry. I didn't see who left it. It was just sitting on the desk with your name on it."

"When did you notice it?"

"Last night."

"At what time?"

"Right around ten o'clock or so, I think, just as I started my shift. I'm not sure how long it was sitting there. I put it under the desk to give to you this morning."

"As far as you know, you're the only person to have touched it?" Jordan asked.

"Yes, sir. I was on duty last night. My shift ends in about thirty minutes, at seven."

"Do you have surveillance cameras here?"

"Yes, we do. They cover the lobby and the elevators."

"We'll need to have the footage from last night and we'll need you to come down to the station to get yourself fingerprinted."

"Yes, sir. I'll do that after my shift is over. Mr. Samson is our head of security. He can help you."

With a nod to his female counterpart, the clerk led them to the back of the hotel to the security room where they spoke to Mr. Samson and obtained a duplicate DVD of last night's surveillance tapes.

As they exited the hotel to the parking lot, Jordan said, "Let's drop off this envelope with the forensic guys, so it can be fingerprinted. We'll check on the report from the other envelopes, too."

"Okay, that sounds like a good idea. Then later on we can view that video and hopefully it'll give us a clue."

Grace took a deep breath to calm some of the butterflies in her stomach.

Jordan asked, "Are you okay?"

"I'd be lying if I said I was. I'm not looking forward to opening that envelope. But it's an integral part of the investigation, so I'll treat it as such. I know how to compartmentalize."

"That's a good trait to have. Imperative when you're in this type of work. What do you plan to do after we've caught Vulcan and you're free to pursue your life?"

"I'll think about that when this is all over."

"Nice way to tell me it's none of my business?"

"I'm not ready to make any decisions right now. I can't plan for the future when I've got an active case going on right now."

"You will have a future, Grace. I'll keep you safe."

"I'll feel better when we have this guy behind bars and off the street."

They pulled up to the municipal building and parked. Grace could see the black smear where her car used to be. The totaled vehicle had been hauled away. She would have to make time to look for a new car once she received her check, but it might be a good idea to wait until Vulcan was caught. She didn't want another ruined car.

They climbed up to the fourth floor and entered the office space that was dedicated to the task force. Several desks were set up around the large room, and off to the left was a long table with chairs that served as the conference room. Several people were sitting around the table. There was a white box that was open, and the smell of fresh-brewed coffee was in the air.

Jordan headed for the room and Grace followed. When they entered, all the people turned to look at her, including the condescending cop. He gave her a once-over, then said, "There's the little lady. How did you fare last night? I sent you one of our best officers to watch over you."

"You are too kind, Detective Russo."

"Ah, call me Ray."

She knew what she wanted to call him, but she was very sure he wouldn't like it. She gave him a tight smile. A woman approached them. She was quite beautiful with soft blond hair styled in a power cut to her shoulders.

She reached out her hand. "Hi, I'm Faye Grafton, your requisite ADA. It's good to meet you."

"And you."

Grace knew Fire Chief Michael Lawrence very well. He was a bear of a man, but none of the flesh on his big frame was fat. He had a salt-and-pepper flattop he wore clipped neatly. His Texas drawl had diminished over the years he'd lived in Southern California. If she went back to firefighting, he would once again be her boss. He gave her a quick nod then turned away, unable or unwilling to meet her eyes. She wondered what was causing his strange behavior.

The last member of the task force sat at the end of the table. He was biting into a chocolate doughnut he pulled out of the white box. Councilman Jim Lyons looked the part. He was dressed in a slick-looking suit, his hands immaculately groomed, with a distasteful look on his face. Grace believed it had nothing to do with the doughnut he was eating. He neither greeted her, nor paid her much heed.

"Good morning, everyone," Jordan said. "Some of you have already introduced yourself to our new co-leader, Grace Addison."

Grace heard Detective Russo snort and she turned to look at him. He gave her a good-natured grin and a Fonz shrug. She returned her attention to Jordan.

"Grace, did you want to say anything?"

"Thank you, Jordan," she said rising from the seat she'd taken. "Good morning," she addressed the task force members. "I want to tell you that I'm here to do a job. As simple and straightforward as that. The mayor thought I would be an asset to the team. I intend to be. I appreciate that I am surrounded by professionals and it is my pleasure to be working alongside each and every one of you with a clear goal of catching the person responsible for the series of fires in this city.

"In case you don't know, this arsonist has taken some interest in me. Yesterday, the arsonist left me an envelope at my front door, then later blew up my car and left a second envelope. He is a bit upset that I escaped what Jordan and I now believe was a trap the arsonist deliberately set."

"For whom?" Faye asked.

"We don't know who he set the trap for, but I can guarantee you, it was a trap. He chronicled almost the whole incident in pictures."

"Seriously? He got everything on film?" Faye asked. Grace could see that she was calculating how she could use that in court.

"Yes, and last night he left another envelope. It's being dusted for prints as we speak."

"What's inside?" Detective Russo asked.

"I don't know yet. I haven't opened it. Wanted to make sure all evidence was collected before I tampered with it."

Grace noticed that Detective Russo hadn't looked at her when he asked his question. He looked directly at Jordan.

She tamped down her annoyance. "Do you have any information on the first envelopes, detective?"

He once again refused to look at her. With his eyes still on Jordan, he said, "Nada. There were no prints except for Agent Kelly's and the victim's."

Victim… Grace felt her anger ignite. He wasn't even going to give her the satisfaction of addressing her as a member of the task force. She opened her mouth to give him a piece of her mind, but a touch on her arm made her shift her focus to Jordan. His eyes were somber, and he gave her an imperceptible shake of his head.

"That's not the kinda news we want, but there it is," Detective Russo said.

Through gritted teeth, Grace said, "Thank you, detective."

Jim Lyons's booming baritone cut the charged silence. "I want to know when you're going to have answers about my warehouse. I lost a lot of money in that fire. All this pussyfooting around and still no suspect."

"Jim, these investigations take time. You know that," Faye said.

At her chastising tone, Jim shot her a sharp look. "Sure, sure. But there's a ton of evidence to sift through. I suggest you get started on it or I'll have both your butts in a sling." He pulled at his cuffs and rose. "I've got a meeting with the insurance company now."

With that he headed to the door as if he was the reigning CEO and they were nothing but his lackeys.

Grace felt an overwhelming sense of pain and loss. She hitched in a breath. The sensation traveled from her tight throat to her stomach, where it settled like a lead weight. His easy and callous dismissal of the lives that had been lost in the numerous fires Vulcan had set twisted inside her like ribbons caught in a strong wind.

"Councilman!" Grace's low voice vibrated with tension.

Jordan touched her arm again, but Grace shrugged it off. Jim Lyons turned and acknowledged Grace for the first time. His shrewd eyes, devoid of any pity or sympathy, watched her dispassionately.

"I think an education about just how difficult it is to do our job is in order. Fires, of course, have many causes. That's the first challenge. Natural triggers like lightning; manmade ones, whether accidental or deliberate; hosts of mechanical, structural, substantive and electrical triggers can all cause fires—and the multitude of triggers doesn't make an investigator's job any easier. Yet by far, most fires originate from human hands, either unintentionally or purposefully. Statistics place that percentage at 70 percent. So that meant the majority of fires are deliberately set by someone with either monetary gain or malicious intent as the motive. Fire is indeed insidious.

"The next challenge for crime solvers is the destructive power of fire itself, let alone any explosions that might occur as a result. It compromises evidence from the start. The longer a fire burns and the larger and hotter it becomes, the less evidence remains. Now add water and the force of hoses used to fight fires and the trampling feet of firefighters, other fire officials, rescue workers, utility company personnel, policemen, safety officers and investigators. The presence and work of so many people raises the risk of contaminating and destroying evidence. Additionally, saving lives always takes priority over preserving a crime scene, and evidence is often sacrificed."

Saving lives was the first rule she learned as a firefighter. It was, as she told the councilman, her focus now.

"Consequently, investigating fires and explosions is both delicate and complicated. Without extensively examining every detail of the scene, gathering data, running tests and conducting interviews, we can only guess at the cause. And a good investigator will never venture any guesses without solid evidence. Determining cause is simply too complex and the consequences of being wrong too great.

"So if we hurry, we risk the chance of being wrong or, even worse, missing something important. Being methodical and deliberate are better choices. When we find out who is doing this, we want to make sure the evidence is strong enough to send the arsonist to jail for a very long time."

And if he didn't come peacefully, then she'd have to put a bullet in him. Somehow, that seemed like the better alternative.

"People's lives are at stake here. People have died. I lost two good friends and colleagues. I don't intend to lose any more," Grace said.

"Well..." Lyons blustered. "See that you don't." He turned and left.

"Peach of a guy," Grace said under her breath. She turned back to Jordan. "I totally see what you mean about Councilman Lyons."

"That's the first time I've ever seen him flustered. Well done."

She didn't want to admit that it mattered what Jordan thought. But it did matter, a great deal.

The meeting broke up and Grace looked at Jordan. "Where are the files from all of the arsons you've cataloged so far?"

Jordan walked to a closed door. When he opened it, Grace saw filing cabinets lined against one wall, boxes situated near them and a rack of neatly labeled evidence boxes.

She undid the cuffs of her pink button-down shirt and rolled them up.

"It's going to take some time to sift through all this material," Jordan said.

Grace nodded. "Then I'd better get started." She walked up to the rack. "Evidence?"

"Yes, everything we've collected, including fragments of the Coke cans and the ignition devices down to any scrap of paper we found at the scene."

"What are these?" Grace asked, picking up a large printout.

"Those are duty rosters of officers on patrol. We pull one for each fire so we can conduct interviews with anyone who might have been in the vicinity of the fires. And, of course, any first responders."

"Can I have access to a computer?"

"Sure," Jordan said. He led her out of the evidence room, through the conference room to one of the desks. "You can use this desk."

"Thank you." Sitting down, she turned the computer on and used her city employee passcode to log on.

"Before you get started, let's take a look at that security DVD we got from Samson," Jordan said, standing next to her.

Sun streamed in through the window and Grace looked at the street outside the municipal building. She watched the passersby come and go as the computer beeped its readiness. She was determined to protect them all.

He set the DVD into the tray and brought up the player on the computer. He fast-forwarded the tape to last night, stopping at seven o'clock. Numerous people approached the desk for various reasons, but neither Grace nor Jordan saw anything suspicious.

At approximately 10:15, Tom approached the desk. He spoke to the clerk briefly then left. Several minutes later someone walked up to the desk in dark clothing and a hat, obscuring his eyes. The man was turned away from the camera. The clerk was busy with a customer and, as slick as you please, the man slid the envelope onto the counter and walked off.

"Clever bastard. He had his face turned away from the camera the whole time."

Grace felt a chill travel down her spine. There was something…familiar about the man on camera, but she couldn't say what. It could be that she was seeing something where there was nothing.

Jordan must have seen something on her face. He asked, "Do you recognize anything about him?"

"Not really. He seems…familiar but…" She shrugged.

"Hopefully, it'll come to you." Using the mouse, Jordan closed the player window and pulled up a directory. "All the evidence we've collected so far is in these files, along with tables and charts."

"What about the duty rosters and the fires? Have you done that correlation yet?"

"No, not yet. We were getting to it but, as I'm sure you're aware, we don't have a whole lot of clerical help. We have one dedicated person and she's overworked as it is."

"I'll work on it after I get acclimated to the system and read through all the evidence."

"Okay, that sounds like a plan. I'm going to finish cataloging the evidence from the Lyons Warehouse fire."

Grace nodded. "Sounds good. I for one wouldn't want my butt in a sling. Sounds painful."

Jordan shifted his weight and turned toward her more fully, his shoulders filling up way too much of the rapidly shrinking space between them. She felt his hot gaze on her and was completely helpless not to turn and gaze directly back.

Jordan chuckled, but it didn't diminish one whit the heat in his gaze. "Yeah. But I think he was the one who got his ass handed to him on a silver platter."

It was Grace's turn to smile and Jordan's grin blossomed and spread as they shared the amusement, the tension between them tightening.

His dark gaze dipped to her mouth and her heart went crazy again. His eyes darkened, stayed on hers, and her heart stumbled into her throat. He leaned closer, so close she inhaled the heat of his skin, felt his restless energy throb in the air. "Yell if you need anything."

"I will," she said, taking a quick and much-needed breath. The man had a way of sucking all the oxygen from the room when he was near her. She pulled up Jordan's first report, tried to forget how those dark eyes had seemed to look deep inside her and started reading.

Jordan's skill in report writing was evident. He listed the facts and what evidence he'd collected and any insights or notes he thought would be helpful. She found herself engrossed in each report. As an arson investigator in training, Grace was aware of the challenge they faced.

She looked up from her computer to find Chief Lawrence staring at her.

Even as he made eye contact with her, his gaze darted away. Unsettled, she stood, a question forming that she wanted to ask him.

"Chief?"

"How are you doing, kid?" He shuffled his feet. "When the mayor came to me to make the request to add you to the task force, I wasn't surprised. I was worried, though. You've been through quite a bit."

"I appreciate your concern. I always have. You've

been a friend to me when I needed one. You helped me make my way through some of the hassles of being a female firefighter. But don't worry about me. I can take care of myself. I can handle any member of this task force."

"Yeah, that was evident," he said. "I think Jim Lyons is an ass, a grade-A ass."

Grace laughed. "Chief, I want to ask you a question about Sara."

His eyes closed briefly and when he opened them they were filled with a deep, abiding sadness. "What about her?" His tone almost sounded defensive.

"She wanted to talk to me on the day she died. She said it was urgent and she looked very stressed out. Do you know if she was having any personal problems?"

"What kind of personal problems?"

She could tell that he was being cautious. "You know, with her husband?"

He frowned in surprise. "Tom? No, no, they had a very strong marriage. As far as I know, Sara doted on him." Then the chief's eyebrows knitted momentarily. "He has had somewhat of a difficult past, if I remember correctly. Wanted into the fire service, but couldn't pass the tests. He went on to be a cop instead. But I don't think that's where his heart was. But it seems as if he's adjusted okay."

"Seems so. Was there anything at work?"

The chief shrugged, avoiding eye contact again. "Not that I was aware of. Sara was an exemplary firefighter. She wasn't even supposed to be on duty that day. Hmm. That reminds me. After her death, Tom came to see me. He was livid, said I was partly to blame for Sara being there that day. I told him I needed her. You were training as an arson investigator and I was short a man…er…in this case a woman."

"You told him Sara was taking my place. That explains his veiled hostility."

He looked immediately chagrined and worried. "I didn't mean to cause you any problem, Grace. I was trying to explain to him how it happened."

"Not to worry, Chief. Tom has a right to his feelings and it's understandable why he would blame me. But I'm interested in the fact that he didn't know that Sara was on duty that day."

"No, he was blindsided when she died. Said that she wasn't supposed to be there. Seems that he was working the scene. Was one of the first patrols to show up."

"Oh, my God. How awful for him to find out that one of the victims of the explosion was Sara."

"Yeah, that had to be tough. Anyway, I'm sorry about everything, especially about you being stalked. You be careful now. That Agent Kelly looks like a capable man, but it doesn't hurt to be extra vigilant."

"I will, and thank you."

He nodded. "Grace, I meant to mention this to Jordan, but the other day we were cleaning out the storage closet and discovered a box of Richard's notes and photos. There may be something there that could be important to the investigation."

"Richard's insights could be valuable. I'll make sure we come by and pick them up."

After Mike left, Grace pondered what he had said. Mike had answered the question why Tom spoke to her with that undertone of bitterness. Why he dug at her every chance he got in his oh-so-polite way.

Tom Parker was the least of her worries. There was a man out there who planned on killing her—by fire.

She trembled and lost her train of thought, couldn't focus on the report in front of her. The thought of how the fire would consume her made her shiver hard from the inside out. Her skin felt tight and she thought she could almost detect the unmistakable smell of burning flesh.

Her heart leaped in a surge of panic. No one could know how she felt about fire now. Before it had been a foe, something to fight to overcome, to extinguish.

Now it seemed like a living, breathing entity, ready to engulf her, reach out and drag her into its hot embrace.

She took in a deep breath, pushed at the crushing fear that slithered through her as if she was pressing against something hard and unyielding.

A phone rang and she jumped. She tugged in a ragged breath, battled down the panic bleeding her skin of warmth. She had to stop allowing these thoughts to consume her. She was stronger than this. She'd survived and gotten out of that basement alive. She had a chance to right a terrible wrong and bring the man responsible to justice. She couldn't lose it. She had to keep it together or she'd find herself off the task force. She'd be locked up and guarded.

That would drive her mad.

Right then she heard Jordan's voice. He was the one who had picked up the phone. And it soothed her. She had no explanation, no answer. It just happened. His deep voice filtered through her like a balm.

Piece by piece she reset her foundations, rebuilt her wall of armor, fortified her soul.

She turned to see Jordan deep in conversation and she rose from the computer and went over to him.

He hung up the phone and looked at her.

"They finished fingerprinting the envelope we found this morning."

"Any hits?"

"No. The hotel clerk came down to the precinct, so we could eliminate his prints. There were no others on the envelope."

The bottom dropped out of her stomach. "So that means…"

"Yes."

"It's time to open it and see what special present Vulcan has left for me this time."

And as easily as that, she felt her foundations crack. They eroded under her, as if instead of the concrete she thought they were shored up with they were resting on nothing but sandstone.

Chapter 6

Jordan watched Grace's hands tremble as she put on plastic gloves to handle the envelope. Even though no prints were found in the first dusting, the gloves served as a precaution for the outside and as a barrier to the material inside.

She took great care as she peeled up the flap of the envelope, only tearing it slightly. Once it was open, she took a deep breath and pulled the contents out—a picture of her charred and destroyed car with a piece of notepaper clipped to it.

The flames are waiting for you, Grace. So an explosion won't do. Consummation with the flames is the only thing that will elevate you. Soon. Prepare yourself.
Vulcan

"I don't like the way this guy is always so close to you," Jordan growled, peering over her shoulder to read the note.

"You mean to take the picture of my demolished car?"

"Yes, that's exactly what I mean."

"There's lots of ways he can remain concealed, Jordan. No one's going to think anything of a man taking pictures at a crime scene. Could be a lab tech, a reporter or just a curious bystander. That's not a bad thing. Maybe we can catch him that way."

"True, but we need to keep an eye out and be more observant and vigilant."

She thanked the techs in the lab and as she stepped outside the door, she shot him a sideways glance, lips quirking slightly.

"What?" he said. "Did you find it funny I would want to be more observant?"

"No, you remind me of my father. He always told me to be vigilant and observant," Grace said. "It would keep me safe."

Jordan nodded. "There you go—that's good advice."

"It is."

"Did your parents…?"

"My parents are gone. My mother from breast cancer and my dad from a heart attack," Grace said.

"I'm sorry about that. No siblings?"

"No. I'm an only child."

"I have two brothers," Jordan said. "But most of the time, they're no help. My parents live in Los Angeles and I used to go to their house every Sunday for dinner.

Of course, that changed when I was assigned here to the task force."

"Yeah. You know Greg, right?"

"How did you know that?" She wasn't kidding when she said she was an intuitive observer. She'd picked up on their friendship from the brief time she'd seen them together.

"I could tell by the way you interacted with him. There was this underlying sense of familiarity. And there aren't many people who would go to the mayor's house after nine at night. So I guessed that you knew him."

Moving toward the front of the police station, they emerged into the lobby. "We were at the Bureau together. He left and went into politics and I...left and joined the ATF."

She gave him a quizzical, sidelong glance, but didn't question why he hesitated. "I guess one law enforcement agency is pretty much like the next."

"How so?"

"You fight bad guys."

He laughed. "Yes, that's true." He felt a sense of relief that she didn't probe about why he'd left the FBI.

Grace laughed, too.

"It's nice to see that you're *able* to laugh, Grace."

The smile froze on her face at the sound of Tom Parker's voice. The dig was not lost on Jordan.

Grace turned and faced Tom. "Hello, Tom."

He stood slightly hunched over, with a foam cup of coffee in one of his large hands. His other hand was thrust deep in a trouser pocket. His pockmarked face showed the reddish stubble of a five o'clock shadow.

"What brings you to the precinct?" Tom asked. His voice held the tired strains of having worked an overtime shift.

"We're here because I received another envelope from the arsonist. It was dusted for prints before I opened it."

"Yeah, that bastard. I'd like to track him down and kill him with my bare hands." He uttered the words in a quiet voice.

"Just leave the investigation to us, Tom. We'll find him, and when we do, he'll pay for his crimes."

Tom nodded and took a sip from his cup.

"We were just heading back to the task force office."

There was a brief, uncomfortable silence.

"Goodbye, Tom," Grace said, somewhat unsettled by his somber demeanor.

They exited the precinct and headed back over to the municipal building. Grace didn't look particularly happy or relaxed at the moment. Jordan's attention kept sliding over to her as he drove through town. He could see that she was twisting her fingers, yet otherwise sitting perfectly still. Too still, like someone deeply lost in her thoughts.

He wondered what she was thinking about. The arsonist, most likely. But he'd be lying if he didn't admit to also wondering if he was preoccupying her thoughts, as she was his. Thoughts that had nothing to do with arson and everything to do with her. His mind spun back to that moment when she'd awakened from her nightmare. The feel of her barely clad body was something he couldn't get out of his mind. The silky feel of her skin and hair a sensual goad.

He couldn't get his mind to leave it alone. That moment when he'd looked into her eyes and wondered if she was as affected by their forced togetherness as he was. And he wasn't sure he'd be so chivalrous and self-controlled the next time. If there was a next time.

Who was he kidding? He knew damn well he wanted there to be a next time.

"Talk to me, Grace."

She settled more deeply into the seat and shifted her gaze out the window. Her face paled. "I wonder how long he's been watching me," she said, her tone pensive. "If he saw me struggling and in pain. Somehow I feel more violated by that. He doesn't have the right. I'm almost more afraid of seeing pictures of myself during my recovery than anything else."

He didn't pull any punches. Grace wouldn't want him to. "He's a predator—there's no doubt about that. But if he does have those pictures, Grace, you'll have to weather that, as well."

Color flooded back into her cheeks, but he couldn't have said if it was from anger or guilt. "I'll weather it, Jordan. Make no mistake about that."

So she was angry because his words once again showed his distrust in her and that he hadn't been very supportive. But he was trying to toughen her up, make her understand that she needed to put her feelings of being a victim aside. He knew that was her goal, as well. But he also knew that anyone in Grace's situation would feel vulnerable. The trick was not letting the arsonist get the upper hand.

"Grace, I was just trying to—"

"I know what you were trying to do. I don't want your sympathy or your platitudes. Your honesty is refreshing. I just wish you would believe in me and my ability to handle this situation." She hadn't said it unkindly, but she was distancing herself from him as fast as she could, without looking panicked about it.

She focused her attention on the road, but something about the arsonist's message to Grace was bothering him. His tone quiet, just loud enough to be heard over the rumble of the engine and the road noise of the big SUV tires, he said, "Consummation with the flames is the only thing that will elevate you?"

She was quiet for so long that he didn't think she was going to answer. At the moment he was more concerned with finding a way past the sturdy walls she'd erected. Or were they walls he had helped to fortify? But it was also a way for him to maintain his distance. Ultimately, he was more concerned about figuring out what was going on—and, if possible, doing something to fix it— than he was about whether she'd still like him when all was said and done. He cared enough at this point, though God knew why, when she was such a contrary thing. He was more concerned about getting this case wrapped up and him away from temptation.

Which begged the question…how was he going to resist that temptation? The more time he spent with her, the more he wanted her. But he had demons of his own to slay. He was still pondering the rather surprising answer to that when she interrupted his thoughts.

"It's part of Vulcan's edict," she said, paused, then ultimately fell silent again.

"It's a threat. I understand that. He intends for you to realize your potential. He intends for you to die by fire and not an explosion."

She gave an impatient sigh, but he noted that her hands tightened in her lap until her knuckles turned white. "I find his behavior…strange. First he sets fires with no notes, nothing is given to us as clues. It's just the act of setting the fires. Now I'm getting these notes."

"What are you getting at?" he asked, turning into the

parking lot in front of the task force office and killing the engine.

She turned toward him. "What changed? What changed to make him target me?"

"You survived the fire," he offered, but even as he said the words, he was sure there was something else there, hidden and tantalizingly close. The fire that almost killed Grace changed the game plan.

"It wasn't a fire exactly. It was an explosion." As she gave voice to her ideas, there was a vibrancy about her now that he hadn't seen before.

"Usually he uses explosions to initiate fires." Looking down, she was silent for a moment. "The soda can is specifically his MO. So why would he change that? Most arsonists are incapable of changing how they start their fires."

"Sure, that's true." He popped open his door and climbed out, needing to get away from her, just for a moment, to break the spell, regroup. But instead, he stopped, turned. "What do you think?"

She came around the vehicle and shook her hair free of the ponytail that had been threatening to come apart all evening. It was done artlessly, with no apparent awareness of how damn sexy the action was. "I think this guy was more of an excitement setter. It gave him a thrill to start fires and watch them burn. Pretty run-of-the-mill arsonist. His motivation is clear and easy," she said, massaging her scalp and groaning a little.

A sentiment he could easily second at the moment. He nodded. "Then something happened to change that." His thoughts drifted back to all that hair and untangling each strand with his fingers.

"Yes," she concurred. "You said you thought he had targeted someone the day Richard and Sara died."

"I still think that's a plausible theory," he pointed out.

"Maybe you'd like to share some of your thoughts on the matter?"

"Like what?" He certainly would. In fact, he was quite willing to share a hell of a lot more than his ideas with her. He turned and started walking toward the office.

Grace followed and when she came abreast of him, she said, "Like who you think was the target."

He turned to face her and caught her eyes as they focused just a tad too long on his mouth. His body revved up quite nicely at that unconscious suggestion. He fought to quell the reaction. They had a long night ahead of them. And at some point he had to get back on task. The case had to come first. "I would guess that the target was Richard Moore."

"How did you come to that conclusion?"

"Sara wasn't even supposed to be on duty, so I don't think it was her. You, on the other hand, also weren't scheduled to be on duty. You were still training and all you were supposed to be doing that day was firearms practice. Richard invited you to come and further your education by investigating a scene that was a possible arson. Is that correct?"

She frowned, and she looked adorable doing it. "That's right. So the question then becomes—why did this guy go from a thrill seeker to a murderer? And why is he targeting me now? Is it because I was the one who got away, or is it something deeper? Something we don't yet comprehend?"

He nodded in agreement as they entered the building and headed for the elevator. Jordan sighed when he saw the out-of-order sign. "Looks like it's the stairs for us."

They climbed the first flight of stairs, and Jordan said, "We also have to ask the question that has been plaguing me since I came up with the idea that this was deliberate murder."

"What's that?"

"Why Richard? Murder has very straightforward motivations," he said.

Just then a FedEx man with several boxes balanced in both arms barreled down the stairs. Grace moved to the side to get out of his way and slammed directly into Jordan, pinning him against the wall.

He got a whiff of her fragrance and it only made him want to get closer, get that scent all over him.

Grace smiled and he thought he caught a flicker of... something else before she quickly moved away from him as the FedEx guy passed. That something else, if he wasn't mistaken, had been a purely female response. Could it be that she liked the feel of him against her? He almost wished he hadn't noticed her reaction. He'd told himself he was only thinking about her night and day because he'd been thinking about the case and how she fit into it.

Standing here now, listening to her voice, which managed to be both soothing and no-nonsense, and looking into eyes that were quick to crinkle at the corners, yet easily held his own when challenged...yeah, he was finding his rationale a little harder to hang on to.

His body was finding it even more difficult. But he was a man, after all, so he could hardly be faulted for noticing things like how her thick blond hair curled around her breasts and how that skirt showcased her very fine behind.

"So what do you think?" she asked.

For a moment, he thought she had read his mind. Then he realized that she was asking about Richard.

"Richard was murdered, I think," she added, then gave him a sideways glance. "It could be something as simple as the fact that Richard was the arson investigator and maybe he was getting too close."

"Did Richard share any theories about this particular arsonist?"

They reached the task force office. "No, not at that time, but now that you mention it, the chief said their was a box of Richard's notes and photos that had been originally overlooked. There may be something there that can help us narrow it down."

"All good questions," Jordan said. "I'd also like to understand why you're being targeted. If you weren't the original target, why does our pyro care whether you survived the fire?"

"I think—and this is just a theory—it's the Vulcan connection. As I said, Vulcan wants the material or, in this case, the victim to bond with the fire. But what I find disturbing about this arsonist is that he seems all over the map. Did he murder Richard, and if he did, why is he spouting the 'be one with the fire' thing for me? It doesn't quite gel. But I guess it's up to us to glean the answers. I think it's even more important for me to research all the fires in La Rosa and look for his specific pattern. Once I get up to speed on the reports. I've got a lot more reading to do."

Back at the task force office, Jordan lost track of time as he sorted through the evidence of the Lyons warehouse fire. His conclusions were pretty much the same. This was the arsonist they were after.

He sat back in his chair and stretched. Glancing at his watch, he realized that, although they had broken briefly to pick up something from the cafeteria downstairs, six hours had gone by. As if on cue, Jordan's stomach rumbled.

He looked over at Grace. He could see that she was on the last report. Almost done. He opened his mouth to ask her if she was hungry, but was interrupted by his ringing phone.

"Hello."

"Jordan, this is Mike."

"Hi, Chief. What's up?"

"We had a fire over at 233 Sycamore. Giving you a heads-up to come on over and check it out."

"Grace and I are on our way."

Grace had turned at the sound of the phone and she was already rising from her chair. "What is it?"

"Fire over on Sycamore. Could be an accident or could be our guy. Up to us to determine that. Now I get a chance to see you in action."

"Don't sound so skeptical. I'm good at what I do."

Jordan refrained from even thinking about the implications of that statement.

They wasted no time getting into the SUV and navigating their way over to the fire. When they arrived, they didn't see any flames, but the two-story house, a family residence, was haloed in orange light, the sky murky with smoke.

The scene in front of her was so familiar. The chief was standing in the middle of the street, bent over a radio in his left hand. Grace knew he was trying to hear the voice on the other end because during a fire it was hard to hear anything above the roar of wood giving way and the shouts for more water, more ladders, more axes. Hoses were everywhere and water sprayed through leaks in couplings. Fire vehicles jammed the street.

In a fire she knew what to do and how to do it—get that roof open! Break those windows! Hot air and dangerous carbons will rise up and out of the four-by-four hole. She had a sudden urge to join them. But, she was "fighting" this fire in a different, less concrete way. She was now waiting for it to be over so she could discover clues as to how it happened. And if it had been set by their arsonist, it would be one more fire added to his sentence.

She shifted to open the door and get out, get her notebook and start taking notes, but as she did the smoke shifted and wafted over the SUV. The scent thick in her nostrils, Grace froze. And that day filtered back to her as if she were actually living it all over again. The sensation was eerie, as though looking at a ghost reliving events. She could smell Richard's aftershave; hear him laugh at a joke as they went inside the house. Inside it was pitch-black. Tables, clocks, a phone. Books, a couch. All these things shifted in and out of sight, materializing through touch and the weak, unreliable light of a flashlight. The light was thin and fragmented wildly so the beam looked like a long narrow sieve though which darkness fell easily.

All her senses were heightened, every nerve ending humming. She was on a mission to find the cause of this fire. What had started it? They went to the kitchen first, because that was the place where many fires started. There they saw the stove was black and charred, darker than anything else in the room. When she bent down to sniff, she caught a whiff of gasoline. Carefully she took a sample, turning and seeing Richard's beaming look at her initiative. Well, he was either proud of her or he was thinking he could retire knowing someone competent was on the job. That boat in Key West beckoned.

She smiled back and nodded. Then she saw Richard frown and lean forward as if puzzled by what he saw. She remembered he said, "Doesn't look like this was much of an effort. Only the kitchen and basement seem to be affected." Then she saw it, a trail on the floor.

Following it, they made their way back into the living room. Grace remembered seeing the open door to the basement. Smart to leave it open so the smoke could ventilate.

Richard was ahead of her and Sara had just entered the room. She smiled at Grace and moved toward her. Grace was surprised to see Sara. She wasn't supposed to be on duty. That's when she came up to her and said, "I need to talk to you. It's really important. Do you have time after my shift?"

Grace nodded, keeping her eye on Richard as he hunkered down and reached out to move some debris.

Then her world exploded. Richard flew at them, his body carried by the blast, both hitting them and shielding them. He caught Sara on the side of the head and Grace in her full midriff and pushed them through the door to the basement. The house rumbled, weakened by the fire that had just flashed through. The stairs gave way and all three of them tumbled down, hitting the basement floor with a crushing concussion that took her breath away and made every bone in her body ache.

A knock on the window snapped her out of her flashback and Grace shivered at the remembered pain, her body pulsing.

"You can't investigate in there."

Grace shot Jordan a sour look. "I know that. I was thinking."

"Looked to me like you were doing more than that. Are you okay?"

"I'm fine," she said dismissing her fear and panic as it curled and twisted in her stomach like a kaleidoscope. Jordan looked at her more intensely. The man had a way of scrutinizing her to the point where she felt he was probing deep inside her.

Fear. It had been her enemy long before she'd almost died in that basement, holding on to Sara's dead hand.

Firefighters never talked about fear. They did what was necessary, and she would, as well.

She ignored Jordan's scrutiny and approached the chief. "How's it going?"

"Ready for you to go in. We've knocked it down and done overhaul, so we're about done."

Grace nodded. She returned to the SUV and went to the back where Jordan had stowed her gear and his. They suited up in protective overalls and boots, both donning gloves.

The fire helmet he placed on his head only lent him a more sexy air. She took a deep breath and turned away, setting her own helmet in place.

Jordan watched her walk away and he couldn't take his eyes off her. Grace had revealed to him what she was hiding and he knew it must be eating at her every day.

She was terrified of fire. He could see it in her eyes as she sat in the SUV and looked at the house. The smell of smoke was a trigger. He was sure she was experiencing flashbacks and that meant she was suffering from post-traumatic stress.

All the more reason she needed to be dismissed from the task force.

With a sigh, he followed her, knowing he had no choice in the matter. Greg wouldn't listen and Grace was too stubborn and too guilt-ridden to quit.

She disappeared into the house as the chief clapped Jordan on the shoulder.

"Is she doing okay?"

"As well as can be expected. She's a tough cookie."

"Don't I know it. I'm proud of her and the way she's conducted herself. Don't be too hard on her."

"I try, Mike, but the fact remains that she should be recuperating, not traipsing around in a husk of a house looking for clues to a serial arsonist."

"I agree, but I'm sure from the tone of your voice you know you have no choice in the matter. Sometimes we do what we have to do."

Jordan nodded and followed Grace inside. She was sifting through debris, her eyes traveling over each piece of material. When she found something, she put it into a small evidence bag. She pulled out a digital camera and took pictures of burn patterns and scorch marks.

When a firefighter walked by, she grilled him on the color of the smoke, what he saw when he approached the fire and any odors he detected. She cataloged everything in her notebook.

Jordan was impressed by her skill, her methodical handling of the debris and her meticulous note taking. He watched every move she made and finally had to admit to himself that Greg Baker might be an idiot for naming Grace to this task force based on political motivations, but he had also appointed a woman who knew what she was doing, even in the face of her fear.

"Jordan," Grace called.

He walked over to where she was crouching. With a pen she sifted through several metallic fragments.

"Coke can," she said.

"So he was here. This is his handiwork."

"Yes." She looked up at him. "We have another fire we can attribute to him."

Grace collected the fragments and she found duct tape and the telltale green lighter.

Back at the SUV, they stripped off their gear and Jordan handed her a moist towelette.

The night was dark and now that the lights had been turned off at the fire scene, the dim glow from the SUV's interior light was welcome. Almost everyone had left, making the place where they stood isolated and…intimate.

"You come prepared," she said, wiping at her neck.

Jordan closed the rear door and faced Grace. He noticed that she had a smudge on her cheek she'd missed. Without thinking, he reached out and wiped it away.

Grace froze; her big blue eyes rose to his and held. The air grew heavy and his chest constricted.

"You did an admirable job, Grace. Even through your fear."

She blinked. "Admirable? Thanks a lot. I did a damn fine job. And I'm not afraid."

"Yes, you are. You might as well admit it to me and to yourself."

"I won't admit anything of the kind because it's not true. What I am sick of is your constant scrutiny. You're always watching me."

Something snapped inside Jordan. He advanced on her, crowding her back against the SUV, getting in her face. "I watch you because I can't keep my eyes off you."

Even as he took her mouth with his, Jordan knew it was the wrong thing to do. And he didn't give a damn. He was finally getting a taste of Grace Addison. And from the moment his lips brushed hers, he knew it was going to be worth the wait.

If he'd planned this, he would have crushed his mouth to hers, overwhelmed them both right off, so neither would have a moment to think or react until it was too late, the deed finally done and out of the way, no longer taunting him with its inevitability. Then he might have had a fighting chance at focusing on the job at hand… and not the hands he wanted to put all over her.

But then there was that little hitch in her breath. And those incredibly soft lips beneath his. And just like that, the image of the tough cookie with the prickly personality was all gone, vanished. In its place burned the image of how she'd been last night. She'd needed him.

That one little hitch…and he'd immediately found himself gentling his kiss, soothing rather than inflaming, caregiving rather than conquering. She tasted so damn sweet. She didn't feel tough. She felt fragile and vulnerable, and damn if he didn't want to save her.

He kissed the corners of her lips before taking her mouth once again. He was unhurried in his exploration, reveling in the moment, knowing it could end at any time with no guarantee of a repeat performance. He kissed her with a gentleness he didn't typically express, and carefully avoided examining any further why that particular side of him had surfaced now, of all times. The fragility he'd sensed was probably temporary at best, no matter what his jacked-up libido wanted him to believe. But he quickly discovered that kissing her like this wasn't just soothing her; it was soothing something deep inside himself, too.

Chapter 7

Oh, damn, the man could kiss. She moaned as those sculpted lips drew on hers. She couldn't stop her reaction to him. It was not in her control—it was primal.

She couldn't say she hadn't wanted to know how it felt to have his mouth on hers. But the circumstances that had brought them together weren't conducive to getting involved.

She had to remind herself that he didn't trust her.

She lost her train of thought when he reached down and pulled her arms around his neck, seating himself more firmly against her.

This was a man who knew what he wanted—bold and aggressive, yet gentle at the same time.

The move was confident, certain and seductive. He didn't just kiss her lips, he feasted on them, and every touch and taste was an invitation for her to do the same. That was something that didn't surprise her about him.

She was a strong, confident woman in bed, but that was before the fire had ravaged her flesh and left her scarred.

The nature of their relationship made this more than recreational sex, more than fun and games. It made her want to react. Her heart squeezed now, engaged despite her wishing it wouldn't be, as he tenderly drew his fingers along the side of her neck, moving his mouth to the delicate line of her jaw, then following the trail of his fingertips.

He'd been gentle with her before. In both his manner and his words. He'd held her when she'd awakened from that terrible nightmare. He certainly had the capacity to protect her.

She had no idea what he was thinking and she suspected not much right now. So much more of her was at risk of being seduced than her body.

She instinctively eased away from him, pushed at his shoulders. It wasn't a shove, she didn't have the strength, still wanting—craving—what he was giving her, but knowing she didn't have the control needed to protect herself. And she wasn't ready to surrender. Not fully.

He stepped back, but only a little, his body still brushed hers. She could feel the heat of him in every pore. She struggled for the clarity of mind she so desperately needed right now.

"I—I," she stuttered, then stopped, willing her head to stop spinning, her legs to stop trembling and her heart to stop pounding. "I can't." She finally looked at him, and his gaze was intense, and as serious as she'd ever seen it.

"I understand," he said quietly and, if she wasn't mistaken, with real regret. He slid his hands to her elbows and eased away. "But I'm a patient man." He touched her hair, his warm palm landing softly on her cheek.

She swallowed against a suddenly tight throat. "I might never—" she began, needing him to know she was making no promises here. She didn't even know what she wanted.

"I know. It's my risk to take," he told her.

She stared at him, into his eyes that held hers so solidly, so certainly. "It's a risk we'd both have to take," she whispered. "You and I."

His gaze hadn't lessened one whit in intensity. He grinned suddenly, his teeth flashing white in the dark. "I like that you're even considering it."

She closed her eyes against the pull of temptation, against the want that spiraled hard and hot through her. She was saved by Detective Ray Russo, of all people, as he appeared from around the bumper of the SUV.

"Jordan…" the sexist jerk said, then trailed off when he saw how close they were standing.

"Hey, sorry. You guys getting a little action under the moonlight?" he said with a laugh. Jordan separated from her, his hands dropping to his side. She felt his shoulders tense and saw his jaw harden. She was aware that Jordan knew who and what the detective was all about, and she saw that he was done with Ray's snide comments.

Before he could say anything, she touched his arm and brought those now hard eyes to hers. "It's okay. I'll handle it."

She walked over to the detective and placed her hands on her hips. "Wow, nothing gets past your amazing detective skills."

"Wha?"

"I'm sure you have some interesting and important

information to share with Jordan. So let's hear what you have to say."

Ray beamed at her, her sarcasm lost on him and his ego. "As a matter of fact, I do."

"By all means, astonish us."

Jordan coughed to hide a laugh, but the detective was too caught up in his information to notice. "A witness stated that she saw a white car here before the fire. A luxury car. She thought it might have been a Mercedes or a Lexus, but she wasn't sure. She said she gets those mixed up all the time, poor dear." His tone held nothing but contempt for the female eyewitness.

"That is very interesting news. Did she get a license plate number?"

"Nope, nothin' that good, but the color and make of the car ain't a half-bad place to start."

"Why don't you get right on that, detective? In fact, it would be very helpful if we had this report on our desks tomorrow morning."

"Wha? It's late."

"But you're a dedicated cop and this information could break the case."

"Okay, I'll have it for you first thing."

When he disappeared, Grace turned to look at Jordan. His eyes were dancing and finally he couldn't contain the mirth any longer.

"I think you made his night. Probably the most praise that poor excuse for a cop has ever received in all his time on the force."

"He deserves it. He's a condescending woman-hater. I hope it takes him all night."

"Did I ever tell you that I love your style?"

"No, but my guess is you only love it when it's not directed at you."

He laughed. "Can't argue with that."

Grace headed toward the passenger-side door and gripped the handle to open it. But before she did she caught the chief's eye. He looked away as if it was too difficult to meet her eyes full-on. He started making a beeline for his vehicle.

"Jordan, just a second," she said as she walked toward the chief.

"Mike," she called out. He only walked away from her faster, as if he hadn't heard her. She caught up to him and said again, "Mike, I want to talk to you."

The chief stood for a moment with his back to her, then turned around. "Sure, sure."

His distant behavior stung. This was once a man she'd laughed and cooked with for hours at one of the firehouse's chili cook-offs. She'd only beaten his excellent chili by a hairsbreadth. She was then crowned Queen of the Chili Makers. And now, now he couldn't even look her in the eye. Did he think that little of her? Was he ashamed of his association with her? Ashamed of her inability to save her colleagues? Her throat tightened.

"I wanted to come by and pick up that box you found."

"That's fine, kid. Just stop by the office and I'll give everyone a heads-up that you're coming." Still he focused on several firefighters rolling hose. Never once did he look at her.

"Mike, what's wrong?"

He seemed taken aback by her directness. "I'm not sure what you mean. I'm just really busy, Grace."

"I feel something is wrong—"

"I can't talk now, Grace. I've got work to do," he said

gruffly. Without another word, he pulled open his truck door and got inside.

"Mike, please."

"There are some things that are better left alone and where to place the blame is one of them."

Shockingly, she felt a sudden burn behind her eyes and squeezed them tightly shut to ward off any ridiculous tears that might think to form there. It was clear that Mike was ashamed of her. Of her actions that night, of her inability to save her friends and coworkers. He was so ashamed of her that he couldn't even look at her or talk about it.

Emotion she'd held in check for so long welled up inside her like a geyser. It rumbled inside her, pressing for release. She wanted to scream her regret and despair into the night sky. But the implications of letting it go held her in check. The risk was too great. She might never get it under control again, might never contain it, and then where would she be? How would she function?

Her heart pumped with sick dread as she turned back toward Jordan's SUV. She glimpsed him behind the wheel, but she didn't meet his eyes. Her hands shook as she grasped the handle of the vehicle and pulled open the door. Inside, the interior light seemed too bright for her eyes. She sat down and closed the door.

She felt Jordan's gaze on her and she sensed that he knew she was stressed. Oh, God, when hadn't she been stressed? It seemed as if she'd been under pressure for a lifetime. She also felt his compassion, something she hadn't felt before he'd kissed her. She didn't want it. Didn't want anyone's pity.

"Everything okay with the chief?"

"I'm not sure," she hedged. "He said we could come by anytime to pick up that box he found."

"Great. We have several things to get to tomorrow, but we'll drop off this evidence and then it's time to call it quits."

Grace nodded. "I need a run before I go to bed and I'm dog tired."

"Then why not skip it?"

"Skip it?" she asked, closing her eyes against the need to run off the shame and sick disgust inside her. "I don't want to. Why don't you take care of yourself, Jordan? I'll take care of my needs."

"Sometimes it's best to let others help."

"How would you know about that? How would you know anything about what I'm going through?"

"I know, Grace."

"Right. You know all about my guilt. Can we just get back, please?"

"Grace, I know you don't want my help and you certainly don't want me to be your bodyguard."

Grace stayed quiet, more because she was denying what Jordan was saying. His presence was becoming soothing and distracting at the same time. She was discovering that having someone to talk to about what happened to her *was* beneficial, she just didn't deserve it. Sara was dead. Richard was dead. Those facts couldn't be changed. And she, Grace Addison, was alive and well.

"Guilt presupposes the presence of choice and the power to exercise it. Survivor guilt may sometimes be an unconscious attempt to counteract or undo helplessness. The idea that you could have prevented what happened may be more desirable than the frightening notion that events were completely random and senseless."

"The event wasn't random. It was planned."

"Doesn't make a difference here, Grace. It's the same outcome."

"I was a firefighter, Jordan. I was trained to handle these types of situations. I had a duty to protect others, and to find a way through obstacles. I failed. I should have—"

"Thinking about what you should have done is counterproductive."

"Okay, so say you do know how I feel. How come you never talk about your past?"

When the silence stretched out, she glanced at him and then looked away just as quickly. Something about the man reminded her of a human package of dynamite waiting to detonate. His jaw was clenched and his hands tight on the wheel. So he wasn't as cool a cucumber as he pretended to be. Somehow that gave her a measure of satisfaction. He seemed so perfect all the time. It was hard to believe he let anything get to him.

"Not so easy, is it?" she said.

"We're talking about you here, not me." The tone of his voice made her edgy.

"Play much ball?" she asked.

"What?" he said.

It was so much easier to reach for anger when she felt fear. "That was a nice dodge. But dealing with this stuff takes time. I'm due my time."

"I agree with that, but not if it interferes with the investigation," Jordan pointed out.

"I wouldn't do anything to interfere with the investigation."

"Including keeping your distance from your fellow investigator?"

Grace was determined to keep the shakiness from

her knees, to keep her guard up. The weakness in her limbs must have spread to her mind. That could be the only explanation for the way she'd clung to Jordan in the dark, his mouth hot on hers, unwilling to let go. The same weakness had her longing to be back in his arms again.

"Especially that. It would be a complicated mess."

"I got it. You don't like messes."

"No. They have to be cleaned up. Best not to make them in the first place."

It took another hour to drop off the evidence to the lab and get it all cataloged before they stopped and picked up a quick bite to eat.

By this time, Jordan was beat and he wasn't looking forward to a run. To his relief, Grace indicated that she was just too tired.

Jordan retreated to his room but, as before, left the door cracked between them.

He yanked off his suit coat and threw it at a chair, not caring where it landed. He felt…frustrated. He tried to tell himself it was about the investigation that seemed to be going nowhere. He could tell himself that, but it wasn't working. He knew why he was frustrated and it had everything to do with the woman in the next room.

He settled on the bed and turned on the TV. For the news, the drone of the anchor's voice buzzing in his ears.

And he drifted, thinking about the warm, moist softness of Grace's mouth on his. The fevered moan that hummed against his lips when he'd opened his mouth over hers. The feel of her silky hair beneath his fingertips, the sensitivity driving him wild.

He slipped into slumber, shifting in his sleep as the warmth of Grace receded. He shivered immediately, knowing where he was. Blood soaked the carpets, spatters against the desks and the wall, dark red like an angry bruise. The smell of it was thick in his nostrils, a smell he didn't think he would ever forget, thick and metallic.

His hands shook, a weakness stealing over him as blood seeped from a wound in his shoulder. Sprawled against a desk pushed up against a window, Dan sat, his FBI-issued Glock hanging loosely from his hand.

"You can't stop me, Jor. You can't stop anything. Make anything better! Don't you get that? Don't you get it?"

Jordan had taken numerous classes in how to soothe an angry hostage-taker. He'd logged countless hours negotiating with men who were on the edge of reason, and in this case he'd failed utterly in his duty to his fellow agents and to his best friend.

"Don't," Jordan whispered.

But Dan only gave a brief laugh. "It's what I came here to do." Slowly he raised his weapon.

Jordan jerked away from his blood-soaked nightmare, his breathing labored as if he had taken that run.

A noise jerked him up in bed and he went to the cracked door. Quietly, he opened it.

Grace wasn't in bed. In fact, she hadn't even pulled the spread down. Softly, he called her name. There was no answer.

Jordan reached into his holster and pulled out his gun. With the barrel pointed down, he entered her room. There was no one there, but he heard something from the bathroom and he went to investigate.

He called her name again and there was no answer. With dread he pushed the door open and froze.

Grace was just emerging from the shower, wrapping a towel around her damp skin.

With a gasp, her eyes widened when she saw his gun and he put it away immediately.

He heard a small sound, then Grace laughed suddenly in the small room. If sunshine had a sound, it would be Grace's laughter.

She braced herself on the edge of the toilet and laughed harder, saying between peals, "The look on your face…"

He chuckled, too, feeling like a complete idiot.

"I thought you were in danger."

For some reason, that only made her laugh harder. She clutched her stomach. Finally, her laughter subsided and she wiped her eyes.

"Nope, I'm not in any danger, but you are."

"Oh?"

"You're in danger of making a complete fool of yourself."

He dropped his chin, and swore under his breath. "I don't know what the hell to think anymore. You're driving me crazy."

"Good. A little payback never hurt anyone. You drive me crazy, too."

It was times like this that made Grace eminently seductive. When her defenses were lowered and glimpses of the way she must have been before Sara's death peeked through, he was utterly captivated. The contrast aroused primitive emotions far better left suppressed.

Seeing the expression on his face, her smile faltered, faded. There was something raw in the way she looked at him, something suggesting hot sin.

Desire swirled in his veins. He wished he didn't have an exquisite memory of her mouth, her scent, the feel of her hands in his hair, seeing those eyes blaze until they reflected nothing but him. If only he could deny the power there was in being wanted, with just that kind of intensity.

A breath shuddered out of her. Her eyes caressed his sculpted mouth.

Their mouths touched, eliciting a soft sigh from both of them. And Jordan sank into a sensuous place that made his flesh sing and his heart skip a beat. The pleasure of it soaked into his skin, and awareness receded, to be replaced with want.

Jordan cupped her face in both hands and feasted on her lips. Hunger sizzled through him, igniting his blood. He followed the enticing seam of her lips with his tongue, coaxed them open. And when they did, need rose up, edgy and fierce.

His arms went around her, dragging her closer and she obeyed his urging. She settled against him. All the while their mouths moved in unison, breath mingled. She touched his chest where it was bared, and the feel of her touch spiked his heart. Her fingers went to the buttons on his shirt, unfastened them one by one. And then went on a sensual discovery, skating over his sinew, bone and hard, hot muscle. Exploring angles and intriguing hollows that made him moan.

He shoved a hand in her hair, pulled her closer. He wanted everything she had to give, more than she'd ever given before. And he wanted, quite desperately, for her to offer it freely. Without reservation.

He dragged his mouth from hers and peppered hard, turbulent kisses along the soft skin of her jaw, to the pulse at the base of her throat. His need to touch her was fueled by the wake of heat her hands left on his skin. Sparks flickered just below the surface of his flesh. He released the towel, skimmed his hand over sensitized flesh.

His world shifted, teetered, and he felt dizzy as her hands rose, fisted in his hair. The contact twisted as unchecked desire escalated to a restless craving. With one gentle finger he traced the swell of her breasts, before cupping one heavy globe in his hand, the point of her nipple hard and demanding against his palm.

She gasped and moaned against his lips, that sound going through him, leaving him hot and aching.

The evidence of her passion sent a hot ball of lust hurtling through him. His hands went to her waist and he pressed her to him, unable to bring her close enough. Need surged from a primal place, desperate and insistent.

His lips closed hot and hard around her, the damp flick of his tongue against her nipple arched her back, bringing her searing flesh fully to him, opening herself to him.

His hand trailed up her arm, to the top of her shoulder and when he felt the rough patch, he stopped.

Grace spun away, grabbing at the towel as she went, pulling it across her body and shielding herself from him.

He saw it on her face—fear. Pure and unadulterated. It smashed his longing with a brutal fist. He didn't know if the emotion was directed at him or at herself. The distinction really didn't matter. The end result was the same.

The bleak realization knifed through him, leaving a sense of desolation that was staggering. He stepped back, wanting to haul her in his arms again, knowing that he couldn't. She was that fragile. That vulnerable. To keep from reaching for her, he turned away to give her privacy. "I'm sorry, Grace," he said, his voice hushed.

Grace dropped her forehead into her hands, as the emotions twisting inside knotted her stomach and pounded at her temples.

It wasn't that she no longer had the will to resist the man. She just failed to recall the need to.

Drawing deep breaths, she fought for control. A control that had been noticeably absent while she'd been in Jordan's arms. A control that, if she was truthful with herself, had been receding fractionally for some time.

Only an hour ago she'd been congratulating herself on her ability to work side by side with Jordan without any personal complications rising between them. Complications. A wild laugh welled up in her throat. What a word to describe what had just happened. She didn't even understand it herself. How was she supposed to explain it to Jordan with the perfect face, perfect teeth, perfect body and perfect skin?

And now it appeared as though she'd deceived herself yet again. Because it was becoming glaringly apparent that she couldn't be near Jordan Kelly for any length of time without her defenses crumbling, one tiny bit at a time. A man who could so easily dismantle her careful guard, thread his way past her resistance, was more dangerous than any fire she'd run into. More dangerous, at least, to her.

Chapter 8

Jordan awoke; the fire Grace had ignited in him yesterday had dwindled down to a slow simmer. Half the night was spent wanting her and the other kicking himself for acting like a blundering fool. An ice-cold shower relieved the first condition, but not the second.

He donned a crisp white shirt and chose a tie to match the dark brown suit, one speckled with tan and turquoise. As he knotted it, he agonized over the misstep he'd made last night. It was the hesitation when he'd reached her shoulder and touched the rough skin. He was so caught up in her incredibly soft mouth, he wasn't thinking with all cylinders. If he had been, he would have handled it differently.

He reached down and grabbed his holster. As he touched the leather, he chuckled, remembering the way she had laughed last night. He'd like to see her laugh like that again and often. A woman as vibrant as Grace should.

He slipped in to the matching suit jacket and went to the connecting door. The clean, flowery scent of Grace drifted into his room from the crack in the door. He breathed her in for a moment. He knocked, and at the sound of her firm, "Come in," he entered.

She was standing near the bed. She'd chosen black slacks cuffed at the ankle that hugged her hips and small waist, a waist his big hands had circled last night. She had on a lime-green short-sleeved blouse that accentuated her creamy skin.

"Ready to go?" he asked.

She met his gaze squarely. "Yes, we'll need to make time to go to the station house and pick up Richard's notes. I'm eager to go through them."

He decided to proceed as if it were business as usual. He wasn't giving up—not even close—but she was clearly in retreat-and-regroup mode. Pushing someone when she's scrambling often worked to break down that resistance, at least enough to get her to the point where she'd ask for help. But he knew that with someone like Grace, that strategy would only make her rebuild those defenses twice as fast, and twice as sturdy. Now was the time to back off and do a little regrouping of his own.

After getting a bite to eat, they arrived at the task force office. Grace went directly to her desk and booted up her computer. Jordan called the lab and told the techs he wanted to be notified immediately when all the tests were done on the evidence they'd dropped off yesterday.

Shortly before noon, Jim Lyons came into the office. He heard Grace say, "Councilman, I'd like a word with ~ou."

"Who are you again?" he asked, cocking his head as if he couldn't quite place her.

"Grace Addison."

"Right, you're the firefighter who almost died in that terrible fire a couple of months ago. You lost two good coworkers that day, right?"

"That's right."

"What do you want to talk to me about?"

"Could we speak in private?"

"Whatever you have to say can be said here."

"I'd like to know where you were the night 233 Sycamore Street was torched."

"What?"

"Your whereabouts. It's a simple question."

There was a long pause as he stared at Grace, his eyes narrowed. "I don't believe that's any of your business."

"Yes, it is. Anything to do with this case is my business."

"Why are you asking me for this information?"

"A white luxury car was spotted at that location. You drive a white Lexus, Mr. Lyons." Grace's tone was devoid of any emotion or inflection.

"So what if I do? I don't see how that's important to you."

"It's important to this investigation, and therefore, it makes it important to me. Could you please answer the question?"

Jim laughed derisively and pointed a finger at her. "You really have a lot of time on your hands, don't you? Are you that desperate that you have to insinuate some kind of impropriety on my part?"

"And what impropriety is that, Mr. Lyons? Enlighten me."

Jim laughed again—this time it was ugly. "You really are a piece of work, you know that?"

"Look, councilman, it's a simple question. Will you answer it or not?"

"I will not. You have some crazy notion that is a waste of your time and mine. I'm a busy man, unlike you, evidently. I have to go."

Jordan watched as Jim Lyons hotfooted it out of the task force office. He didn't even wait for the elevator—he headed for the stairs.

"Grace…"

She turned toward him, her eyes flinty. "Did you know the councilman drove a white luxury car?"

"Yes, I did."

"Why didn't you look into him after he lost his third building?"

"I didn't have any evidence that pointed to him. And a white luxury car isn't compelling evidence, Grace. A defense attorney will chop us off at the knees with that kind of evidence."

"That's why you're going to drive me over to the courthouse so I can get a warrant to look at his financials."

"You're going to pull his accounts?"

"Yes, I am. And I will dig further if that's what it takes."

"This is going to have some fallout. I hope you know that."

Grace shrugged. "I'm not afraid to step on some toes if it gets me the answers I'm looking for. How about you?"

"No, I'll back you up on this one. I think it has merit."

"Oh, no, be careful, Jordan. It sounds like you might be trusting me."

The renovated courthouse with its impressive columns

made Grace proud of her pursuit for justice. Inside the cool interior, Jordan and Grace took the elevator up to ADA Grafton's office. Faye's office looked like any typical hardworking ADA's. Files covered most of the available surface of her desk. Her diploma from Columbia was framed in wood and hanging directly behind her.

"Have a seat. What can I do you?"

"I need a warrant for Jim Lyons's financials."

Faye took on an expression that was a mix of dismay and shock. "What? Why?"

"Last night there was a fire and an eyewitness saw a white luxury car parked at the residence before it started. With the fact that there have been several fires at Jim's businesses, I think a warrant is in order."

Faye shook her head. "Grace, you're making a mistake. Jim isn't capable of doing such a thing."

"How do you know that?"

"I know. Can't you take me at my word? I know what I'm talking about."

"Faye, we can't just let this ride. There are too many questions that need to be answered. I'm afraid I can't budge on the warrant."

"Can I speak to you both off the record?"

"Depends on what you have to say," Jordan said.

Faye gave Jordan a severe glance. "This is a delicate matter," Faye replied. "I would appreciate if you'd keep this information confidential."

Jordan looked back at her, making no promises.

Faye rubbed at her temples, clearly irritated. "Jim and I are seeing each other, and he was with me that night. Believe me, I have no illusions that he was trying to protect me in any way. It's no-commitment sex for me."

"When did you leave the residence?"

"About eleven."

"Then there is some question as to whether or not Jim set that fire. I determined that it was set between eleven and twelve."

Faye compressed her lips and shook her head. "I still can't believe Jim did it."

"You deserve better, Faye."

"Thank you, Jordan, for saying that. Jim doesn't want his wife to find out."

"He called you?" Grace asked.

"Yes, and he's very agitated."

"I'll bet he is," Jordan said, seating himself in one of the chairs in front of Faye's cluttered desk.

"Where was the fire?" Faye asked.

"At 233 Sycamore."

Grace saw the recognition and dismay in Faye's eyes. "That's where you meet." Grace stated it as a fact.

Faye leaned back, concern lining her face. "Yes, Jim owns it. He bought it just for our affair."

"Sounds like he's knee-deep in something here," Jordan said.

"Jim didn't do it."

Grace leaned forward, her eyes sympathetic. "I'd still like a warrant for his financials, Faye. We have to check out our leads. You must understand that."

"I do. But even though Jim might seem like the obvious suspect, don't overlook other connections."

"What connections do you mean, Faye?" Grace asked.

"The SCBA connection. This case has stumped me. There are so many different confusing aspects. I've been an ADA for a long time, but I've never seen a case like this one."

"I understand fully, Faye," Grace said. "People who

commit crimes have motives for what they do. I think we need to take into consideration a strong motivation in this case."

"Which is what?" Jordan asked.

"Revenge," Faye said. "We aren't ruling out the fact that Richard Moore and Sara Parker could have angry relatives and I think that has to be taken into consideration."

"There's the explosion itself, which wasn't Vulcan's traditional MO. Only after Grace survived does Vulcan materialize. Now he's targeting her. There's an explanation for all of this—I guarantee you," Jordan said.

"But I think you're looking at the wrong suspect," Faye insisted.

"Thank you for your insight, but I'll need the warrant. If you feel that it's a problem for you, we can ask another ADA."

"No. I'll carry out my duty to this office. I think Judge Carter is in her office. Give me thirty minutes."

Faye came back in twenty and handed Grace the signed document.

"Judge Carter balked at signing at first, once she found out it was for Jim, but I explained to her why you were requesting the warrant and what evidence you had to back it up. She reluctantly signed."

"Thank you, Faye."

"Be careful, Grace. Sometimes the most obvious explanation is just a smokescreen."

As they drove away from the courthouse, Grace tucked the search warrant in her purse.

"Let's head over to Station 65 to get Richard's notes."

He nodded. "That was quite the revelation."

"Faye sleeping with Jim Lyons? There's no accounting for taste. Sure, the man is handsome, but there's something oily about him. I know he's mixed up in this somehow. Whether he's a victim? I'm not sure about that."

"It's good to keep your options open. We haven't arrested him yet. He and the mayor are as thick as thieves. Greg is going to be concerned."

She wanted to be mad at him, even though she realized it was just an excuse to focus her feelings of helplessness on something tangible. Or someone. Instead, she took a deep breath and let it out slowly, forcing herself to relax back against the seat. Getting worked up wasn't going to help matters any. Besides, she'd already gotten worked up quite enough. She glanced across the seat, to where Jordan's hand rested on his thigh.

His hands were wide, the fingers long and tapered. And there wasn't anything wrong with that thigh of his. She swallowed another urge to sigh, only this time she was afraid it would sound more wistful than weary. He'd put his hands on her, his mouth on her... Her heart kicked up just thinking about what had happened last night. Yes, she was tired and scarred and worried about everything…but that wasn't the reason her pulse was racing and her palms grew damp.

No, she could lay this unsettled, edgy feeling right at the cowboy boot-clad feet of her bodyguard/partner.

They turned onto the street where the station was housed. When they pulled up in front of the station, Jordan cut the engine and went to open his door.

Grace reached out and touched his arm. "Jordan, wait. I need to ask you a favor."

He looked down at her hand and she removed it, her palm tingling.

"Shoot."

"I want to go in alone."

"Grace…"

"I know. You're not too keen on that idea. I need to speak to the chief alone. It's personal. Besides, I'll be surrounded by burly firefighters. Nothing will happen to me. You'll be right out front. All I need is fifteen minutes, twenty tops."

"I don't like it."

"Believe me. I can tell you don't. You take guarding me seriously. I appreciate that."

"What was that?" he said as if he hadn't heard her. He put his hand to his ear and leaned forward with an expectant look on his face.

"I said I appreciate it."

"Can I get that in writing?"

She laughed and his eyes crinkled at the corners when he smiled. Damn, why was that so sexy?

"Ah, there's that laugh. It looks good on you."

"Very funny."

"I'm serious. I think I have some paper in here and there's a pen somewhere."

"Jordan," she said, smacking him on the arm.

His lips curled fully then, and in his smile was all the reassurance she found she needed. "I'll give you fifteen minutes, then I'm coming in. Nothing is going to stand in the way of this assignment."

There was the tiniest pang, then, at the realization that this was temporary for him. When it was over, he'd be going back to LA, which was ridiculous, as she'd barely gotten used to the idea of him being here in the first place. She should feel relief that perfect Jordan Kelly would be gone and no longer judging her. So what she did next didn't make any sense. "I do like a dedicated agent," she said, her gaze dropping from his eyes, to his mouth, then forcibly back up to his eyes again. If the way his pupils slowly expanded was any indication, he hadn't missed the slip. But then she'd bet that he rarely missed anything.

"Do you now?" he asked, his voice a shade rougher.

"Yes, shows commitment."

His grin was slow, confident and downright devastating to her already engaged libido. What was she thinking, taunting him like that?

His throat worked, and her pulse shot up. "Nothing wrong with self-preservation," he said, his eyes dropping to her mouth, consuming her for a long moment, the hungry look stirring her blood, then slowly moved back up to hers.

Didn't she learn? She couldn't spar with Jordan without putting herself in yet another dangerous predicament, but the potential outcome of this one didn't give her a tension headache; it made her muscles tighten in the sweet ache of anticipation. This was an entirely different, rather delicious sort of tension. "I know how to take care of myself, for sure. The last couple of months have been quite an education."

The man was definitely getting under her defenses. All of a sudden, she wanted to know how it would be to lean on someone. Cede all her cares and just let go. She knew how sensitive Jordan could be. He'd shown her countless times. But how forgiving would he be of her scars?

The very fact that she was flirting with him made her suddenly feel guilty. Sara would never have a chance to flirt with her husband again or let her cares go or lean on him. She couldn't even count on Grace to save her when it mattered most.

"I guess you would have, being a firefighter. It's a tough profession and you, Grace, are one tough cookie."

"Well, this tough cookie is going to get going and pick up those files and talk to the chief. I'll be right back."

He lifted a hand as if he was going to caress her cheek, and she held her breath but didn't move away. He checked the motion at the last second, let his hand fall back by his side. She had to work at not letting her shoulders slump in disappointment. He moved back, putting more distance between them.

Distance she found she didn't like all that much anymore. Even with that undercurrent of tension, she'd actually relaxed. She wondered if he'd purposely driven the conversation that way just for that reason. It made her want to lower her guard with him. Made her want to believe that engaging him in a little harmless flirtation was simply an exercise in taking her mind off her troubles. Except he was trouble. And there was nothing harmless about him.

Before she got herself into any more trouble, she made her escape from the vehicle and crossed the street. As she approached the station house, she found herself surrounded by members of her old squad. A lot of them patted her on the back and one six-footer picked her up and swung her around. She laughed so hard she cried.

"Glad to see you, Grace," Charlie Manning, the six-footer, said. "When you coming back?"

"Still healing, so not for a little while," she said and bit her lip. She'd already made her decision.

"Why are you here?" Dave Sanders asked.

"Here to see the chief and to pick up some of Rick's files to see if they'll help with the investigation."

"That's right," Charlie said. "She's a big-shot arson investigator on the task force. When you find that guy, could you give us advance notice?"

"Now, that wouldn't be a good idea, would it, Charlie? We want him to stand trial for his crimes."

Charlie laughed as Grace walked toward the open garage that held the gleaming trucks and emergency vehicle.

The La Rosa Fire Department currently had nine stations—one in each of the city's major precincts. Each year the department responded to more than fifteen thousand calls, ranging from medical emergencies to working fires. The department also had a very active fire prevention division, which offered education for school classes, business safety inspections and, with Rick on the squad, conducted fire investigations.

Inside the cool interior of the garage, Grace paused and took in the boots and turnout pants ready for her coworkers to step into as they raced to a fire.

She entered the kitchen where Peter Smith, known as Smitty, was busy cooking. Memories of all the times she'd helped to cook there and the camaraderie she experienced assaulted her. She and Sara always ate side by side when their shifts coincided. And Rick would keep them all in stitches. In fact, once Charlie blew milk right out of his nose when he made the mistake of drinking while Rick was telling one of his jokes.

With a heavy heart she walked to the chief's office and knocked on the door.

"Enter," he said.

When she walked in, he stood and shuffled his feet. "Grace. I've been expecting you. Got all Rick's stuff boxed up right there. I hope it helps out in some way." He looked everywhere except at her.

"Mike, thanks. I appreciate it. I hope it helps, too."

"Yep." He nodded vigorously and the moment dragged out awkwardly.

"Mike, I'm sorry. I'm sorry I failed in my duty to Sara. I'm sorry Rick died. I should have done something to save her. I should have—"

"Grace, no. Don't say that. You did everything you could, kid. You have nothing to feel ashamed about."

"Then why can't you look at me? Why did you say that about blame?"

"Damn, you thought I was talking about you? Oh, man…" His voice trailed off, and he dipped his head a moment before looking at her. "No. Not you, kid. I was talking about me. It's all my fault. I was impaired that night."

"Impaired?"

"Grace, I was drunk."

"Oh, no, Mike."

"I've been sober since the night you…since the incident. I'm the one who needs to apologize. I hope you can forgive me."

"Of course. I want to forgive myself, too, but I hope that comes with time. Say that it will, Mike."

"Can't say that, but I can promise you when you come back, you'll have a leader who intends to remain a leader."

"That's something I need to talk to you about."

"Grace…"

"I'm not coming back. I can't face it every day with the memories of Sara and Rick. It's too much for me."

The chief's face took on a grim look. "Well, there's no need to make a decision right now, is there? You have some disability coming to you and you're working this task force. Why don't you put off any final decisions until you're ready to come back for duty?"

"I think I've made up my mind."

"I say let's wait. Can you do that? If you feel the same way a couple months from now, I'll accept your resignation. Fair?"

She smiled and he met her eyes and smiled back. "Fair. Thanks, Mike."

He nodded. "Do you need some help with that box?"

"No, I think I can manage it. Jordan is out front and it's not far to walk."

"That's a fine young man."

"He's pushy, judgmental and sees way too much."

Mike chuckled. "Yeah, I can see where that wouldn't sit well with you. Don't be too hard on him."

"I'll try not to."

Grace picked up the box, which wasn't that heavy, and Mike opened the door for her. "I'm glad we talked, kid. I'm sure I'll see you over at the task force office. Oh, and I forgot to tell you. We got ourselves a new addition. It's a Black Labrador for the arsons. An accelerant-sniffing dog. She's a beaut, too."

"A dog. That's great. Should be very helpful in investigations. I'll see you, Mike."

When she approached the kitchen, all the guys from outside were seated around the table. They tried to get her to join them, and every one of them offered to carry her box, but she refused both invitations. Jordan wasn't going to wait much longer.

When she reached the dark interior of the garage, she saw that the big doors were closed. She headed for the side door and, setting the box down, she stepped through. Holding the door with her foot, she hefted the box out and set it on the ground. Before she could turn around, someone grabbed her from behind. He slammed her into the brick wall that bracketed the short alley connecting the two parallel roads that ran in front and back of the firehouse.

Shooting stars exploded in her head and something wet and sticky slid down her face. She was whirled around and a fist hit her, a crushing blow to her cheek, followed quickly by a clip to her chin. Semiconscious, she dropped heavily to the ground. With dimming vision she saw someone with black shoes standing over her. She saw the shoe lift. Then somewhere off to the side and out of sight, she heard Jordan call her name. Her assailant dropped his foot. He quickly picked up the box. The next thing she heard was the sound of a vehicle peeling away from the curb. When she focused, she could see the car. It was white and looked expensive.

Then she fell down into deep, quiet darkness.

Chapter 9

At the sound of squealing tires, Jordan came around the side of the station house. When he saw Grace lying facedown on the concrete, he sprinted to her, calling out her name.

When he reached her, he skidded to a halt, dropping to his knees. "Grace!" His voice was urgent, a vise squeezing his chest. "What the hell happened?"

Jordan pounded on the door. "We need some help out here!" Someone opened the side door then swore softly. Calling inside, his voice boomed and echoed in the large garage. "Smitty, get your equipment and get out here! Someone's attacked Grace!"

Jordan heard several pairs of running feet. She was already coming around when the guy called Smitty came barreling out the door carrying a case. Evidently, he was the resident EMT. Several other firefighters appeared as well, including the chief. "What the hell!" he said.

"Talk to me, Grace, honey," Smitty said gently.

"The arsonist was here. Did anyone see him? He just drove away," she said thickly. Even with the blood covering one side of her face, she looked like an adorable waif as she stared up at all the men crowding around her.

Smitty looked at Jordan. "Let's get her into a sitting position."

Jordan gently helped her up. He dropped to a squat and pulled Grace against his chest. "Lean against me, Grace."

"I'm okay. Just scrambled my brains for a minute."

With a gauze pad, Smitty began to clean the blood off her face. *Blood*. Jordan's stomach lurched violently, his hands clenching in murderous intent.

Smitty cupped her chin and flashed a light back and forth several times in her eyes. He breathed a sigh of relief and met Jordan's eyes. "No concussion. Let's take a look at that cut." He gently dabbed at the seeping wound at Grace's hairline. "Superficial. It won't need stitches. But the side of your face might swell a bit. Need to keep cold compresses over it."

Jordan heard a siren gradually getting closer. A car door slammed, and Tom Parker materialized around the corner of the station house.

"When I got the call on my radio, I couldn't believe it. Grace, are you all right?"

"Yes. I'm fine. Right, Smitty?"

"She is. She got her clock cleaned, but good. She's a tough one, all right. Find that bastard."

Tom shook his head, "You're lucky you weren't killed."

Jordan rose, still supporting Grace. With his hands under her arms, he helped her to stand. When she was fully upright, he couldn't let her go, something urgent and primitive stirred inside him. She leaned into him, and he wasn't sure if it was a result of the weakness in the wake of her attack or whether Grace was finally giving in.

It was one of the most courageous things she'd ever done as far as he was concerned.

He wasn't aware that this alley actually connected the street in front of the firehouse and the back. His fault for being lax in his duty.

Tom took Grace's statement. She couldn't give him much. Just that she'd been attacked from behind, slammed into the brick wall and punched twice. She caught a glimpse of black shoes and black overalls, the kind a mechanic would wear. Her assailant took the box of Rick's notes, valuable in their investigation. The last detail she told Tom was that her attacker was driving a white luxury car. She saw it when it sped away from the curb.

Once Grace was done giving her statement to Tom, Jordan reached for her elbow and began leading her away. "I think we should head back to Faye and get a search warrant for his house," she said.

"For whose house?"

"Jim Lyons's," Grace answered, her expression saying that it should be obvious. "The car, Jordan. There must be something in the notes that he's afraid we'll find."

"We're not going back to the courthouse or the task force right now."

"But why?"

"Do you have a total disregard for your well-being? You were just assaulted! You were facedown on the pavement when I got there. Your face is swelling. You're going to have bruises and I'm sure, if I'm guessing correctly, a massive headache." He opened the passenger door, but she resisted getting in.

Turning to him, she cupped his face. "This isn't your fault."

The warmth of her touch did a lot to thaw some of the ice-cold panic he'd felt. "Whose fault is it?" he said stoically, feeling ten times the idiot for not following procedure.

"It's mine for underestimating the danger I'm in. You, on the other hand, argued with me, but ultimately the decision was mine to make, so don't beat yourself up about it."

"If you insist," he said, the thought of what could have happened to her churning in his gut, making him crazy.

"Jordan," she said softly. "Do it for me." She moved her thumb across his cheekbone and he was completely lost.

The plea in her eyes might have weakened his resolve, but he'd ignored the screeching inner alarm earlier when he'd let her go into the station house alone. He shouldn't have, and once upon a time, in another life, he would have listened to that insistent clanging. This time, though, Grace could have been killed. That, he was sure, would have done him in.

He grasped her upper arms. He wouldn't make any more mistakes, not after he'd pledged to protect her.

"There's a time to take care of yourself."

"And there's a time for justice, Jordan. We can't wait too long to get that search warrant." Her expression softened, compromising. "I'll rest afterward. I promise, but please let's do it now. If we don't find anything, then I'll admit that I was wrong."

He sighed. "Grace..."

"At the very least, let's pull his financials and see if he's even in trouble with money." She withdrew a little. He could feel her shoring up her defenses.

He closed the passenger door on her statement, rounded the vehicle to the other side and got in. The short walk had given him time to tuck away the frustration still simmering inside him. Time to stop wanting to put a fist through the walls she was already trying to rebuild.

They were there, shaky but unmistakable. Most women would have collapsed by now. Most men, too. But Grace couldn't be compared to other people, because of one inescapable fact. She stood alone. Even in her darkest hour, when she'd clung to him for comfort, she hadn't really wanted to.

"It won't take that long. You can get that woman-hater to do it. It'll be faster."

He chuckled against the onslaught. "You must be okay if you're willing to let Ray take some more potshots at you."

"Ray? In a battle of wits, I'm afraid he's weaponless."

Jordan chuckled again. "All right. We'll go and pull his financials, then take it from there."

She reached up, touched the bandage on her forehead and said firmly, "He's going to be sorry he ever messed with us."

At the police station, Ray was at his desk. When he saw Grace, his eyes widened. "Grace! What happened?"

"I was attacked at the fire station when I went to pick up Richard's notes. That's what happened."

"Aw, damn! I remember your mentioning Richard's notes back at the Sycamore fire. Did you see the guy?"

"No."

Ray came from behind his desk. "Here, you sit." He stood over her and eyed her face. "Guy did this right outside the fire station with all them big firefighters milling around? Anyway, he must think he's some tough guy. I wish I coulda been there. If I ever get my hands on him…"

"Ray, it's really nothing…"

"Nothing? Waddya kiddin'? No, that's a lot! A whole lot."

"Just…stop it, Ray. What's with the concern?"

Ray looked at her, his eyes taking on a hurt expression. "We haven't been the best of friends. I'll admit I've been taking potshots at you. But, well, you've got a lot of moxie, Grace."

"Okay, that's fine. We're friends. Can you just stop acting like that?" she said, an edge to her voice.

"Yeah, okay. Whatever you say."

He looked at Jordan, who was standing behind her. Jordan pursed his lips, tilted his head back and spread his arms in a dramatic show of mental anguish toward heaven, like the prophet Job lamenting the difficulties of his life. Grace turned and looked at him, but only saw Jordan looking innocent behind his sunglasses.

"We need you to pull up Jim Lyons's accounts. We have a warrant," Grace said, flashing Jordan a suspicious look.

Ray seemed to completely forgive Grace's hostility for his commenting about her attack, but Jordan was surprised. The man seemed almost conciliatory. Had Grace won him over? That was quite a feat. Grace seemed more annoyed by his concern than by his barbs.

Ray pulled Jim Lyons's bank account statements and credit card statements. It was apparent that the man was in deep financial trouble. Jim would need his wife's considerable bank account to help him out of this one.

"It's clear, Jordan, that he needed the insurance money."

"Yes, it is, but, Grace, let's think this through," Jordan said.

"There's nothing to think through. This was a scheme to make us think there was a serial arsonist at work. Jim needed the money and when Rick got too close, he killed him. That's why he took his notes."

"Sounds like a good reason to me. I'll start the paperwork for a warrant," Ray said thoughtfully, nodding.

An hour later, Jordan, Ray and Grace were knocking on the door of Jim's opulent home in one of the ritzier districts of La Rosa. When a pretty, well-dressed woman answered the door, the shock on her face made Grace feel sorry for her.

She indicated that Jim wasn't home. "You see, ma'am, that's not required. This piece of paper says I can search his place. I'm asking you to move aside," Ray said.

They made their way methodically through the house. Jordan's concern heightened as Grace touched her temple several times. He knew she was experiencing that doozy of a headache he'd predicted. When they reached the garage, they discovered the mother lode. Pulling open a workbench drawer, Jordan found a bag of green lighters. Under a tarp near the entrance to the garage was the box filled with Richard Moore's notes.

"My guess is that Jim's favorite soda is Coke," Grace

said. Ray was already on his radio putting out an APB on Jim. Mrs. Lyons, her face pale, murmured something about calling her lawyer and left the garage.

Deciding that Jim might be at the task force office, all three of them headed over there. When they reached the fourth floor, both Jim and Faye were there, talking in the conference room.

Ray reached back and pulled out his handcuffs as he solemnly approached Jim. His face paled when he saw them and he turned pleading eyes to Faye. "Don't let them do this, Faye."

"Jim…" she said softly with regret.

"James Lyons, you are under arrest for the murder of Richard Moore and Sara Parker and for the attempted murder of Grace Addison. You are also charged with setting numerous fires including three that destroyed your own property. You have the right to remain silent…"

As Ray read Jim his rights and escorted him out of the building, Faye looked at Grace.

"You're making a mistake."

"We found evidence at his residence, Faye. Indisputable evidence." Grace needed to confirm that in her mind. She couldn't shake the sense that this whole capture of Vulcan seemed so…easy. Too easy. But the evidence didn't lie. What they found in Jim's garage would be strong enough for an indictment.

Faye closed her eyes and dropped her face into her hand. "I just can't believe Jim is capable of such unspeakable acts."

"Why, because you think you know him?" Jordan asked.

"No, because I think I'm a fair judge of character and

Jim just isn't the type. I've got to make some calls," she said and left.

Jordan turned to Grace. "How you holding up?"

"I've got that headache you mentioned, but I wouldn't have missed this for anything. Sara and Richard finally have justice."

Jordan nodded. "You feel up to watching this interrogation?"

Grace's eyes gleamed. "Yes, I do."

Back at the precinct, Ray had placed Jim in a small interrogation room. Grace stood next to Jordan in front of the two way mirror as they eyed the broken man sitting at the table. Ray entered the small room.

"This isn't quite what I expected of Vulcan," Grace said.

"Agreed," Jordan said. "I expected more arrogance."

When they opened the door, Jim sat up straighter and some of his arrogance returned. That seemed to give Grace some satisfaction.

"Hello, Mr. Lyons—or, should I say, Vulcan."

Lyons glared. "That's a lie. I'm not an arsonist or a killer. I'm being framed."

"Sure you are, Jim," Jordan said. "We found the lighters and the box you took from Grace this morning. You did a number on her," he said in a steely voice, advancing toward him, making Jim's face pale at the look in his eyes.

"I didn't touch her! So back off, tough guy. I didn't take anything. This is all wrong. You have it wrong."

Ray grabbed Jordan's arm and shook his head. They were playing good cop/bad cop. But she knew deep in her gut that Jordan wasn't playacting. The anger he showed on her behalf was both real and made her feel somehow safe.

Jordan sat across from Jim, opened the first envelope and spread out the photos of her and Sara lying prone and injured, slowly dying from the toxic fumes.

"And these, Jim? Did you enjoy watching these women slowly die from smoke inhalation? Did it give you satisfaction to hold their lives in your hands?"

"No!" he said violently, shoving the photos away from him with a flick of his wrist. "I wasn't there. That isn't me!"

"I don't know what your twisted reasons are for doing what you did, but I would suggest that you get out in front of this now," Ray said.

Jim's eyes hardened. He rested his forearms on the table and leaned forward, his glittering eyes fastened on Jordan's face. "You people are going to pay for this. I'm being wrongly accused and I'm going to sue you. I'm going to sue the city and by the time I'm done with you, the only employment you'll find is holding a cardboard sign begging for bucks."

"Confess to your crimes and maybe it'll go easier on you. Killing firefighters in the state of California gets you the death sentence," Grace said.

Jim's face stiffened, and he settled back in his chair. "Oh, God," Jim said softly, his eyes widening. "You are stark raving mad. I didn't… It wasn't me!"

A lawyer opened the door and said, "This interview is over. Mr. Lyons has nothing else to say."

Mrs. Lyons stood behind the lawyer, her eyes hard and her expression tight.

"Elise. Thank God."

Grace left the viewing room and stood at the entrance to the interrogation room. Jordan was collecting the photos and stood. When he saw her at the door, he paused, then turned back toward Jim.

"A lawyer isn't going to be able to help you," she said quietly. "Sara and Rick will have justice and you will soon be facing that judgment."

The door closed on Jim's angry face.

Now that it was safe for her to return home, Jordan stopped by the hotel and picked up her belongings. Grace was quiet most of the trip over there, but when they got within sight of her house, she relaxed a bit.

"You did a good job, Grace."

She tensed beside him. "We did a good job."

He smiled. "Okay, we did."

"I guess this means you'll be leaving soon to go back to the ATF in LA."

Basically, this assignment was over. The sudden reluctance he felt at the thought of going back to the city surprised him. He would, of course, have to come back to La Rosa to testify once Jim was arraigned and the trial began. But he knew from experience that that could take some time.

"Yes, but not right away. I'm sure Greg's going to want to talk to me and I've got to get in touch with my boss and brief him on the situation."

She nodded. "Another arson?"

He shrugged. "That's a good possibility, but I'm not sure where I'll be going next."

He pulled into her driveway and indicated she should go in. Once inside, he went to check the rooms and remembered he didn't have to. Yet he did it anyway. If it wasn't for the fact that they had found such damning evidence at Jim's residence, Jordan would have thought Jim couldn't have been responsible for the brutal acts against Grace and the other victims.

Everything seemed just too…pat, and that made him uneasy.

"I'm sure you'll want to take a shower. I can fix you something to eat."

Her smile looked forced. "I think I could sleep for the rest of the week."

He nodded. "You'll feel much better in the morning if you shower and get something substantial in your stomach. I think you've been running on adrenaline for most of the day." As she started to protest, he cut her off. "While you're in the shower, I'll get your bags out of the SUV."

He took her hand and pulled her up the stairs. Her head looked like it was really bothering her. "Where do you keep the pain meds?"

"In the medicine cabinet."

He entered the bathroom, opened the cabinet and grabbed the bottle. Shaking three tablets in his hand, he offered them to her after filling her water glass.

She had a bemused look on her face and he said, "What?"

"You are quite the little helper, aren't you?"

"Indulge me, Grace," he said dryly.

She smirked and took the tablets and the water and obediently downed both.

"Happy?"

"Ecstatic. Go ahead and take your shower," he directed. He needed to keep his mind on these mundane things and off the fact that Grace was fully capable of taking care of herself. "I'll go out and get your stuff, then get you something to eat. Something quick," he said, eyeing her critically. He doubted that her appetite was very strong, but she needed fuel.

She took a breath, exhaled slowly. "Thank you for all

you've done." The bruises on her face were beginning to color and he was thankful that she hadn't been seriously hurt. "But you don't have to stay. I'm just going to pass out."

He had no intention of leaving her like this. Adrenaline had a way of making a body pulse with tension. Grace had already been through a lot and the strides they'd made seemed to dissolve as she pulled her armor around her.

She had an amazing capacity to process traumatic events, but the thought of him staying here put her completely on edge. She looked more shaken about him playing nursemaid than when he'd found her lying with blood all over her face in that alley.

After Jordan had retrieved Grace's belongings, he set her bags in her bedroom. The shower was still running and he thought that was good. She was taking advantage of the hot water to relieve some of the stress she'd endured and tried to compartmentalize, and it would loosen up her muscles so sleep would be more restful.

He went to the kitchen and riffled through the cupboards. There wasn't much there. He wondered if Grace had to fend for herself after she'd come home from the hospital. The thought of her dealing with both her pain and loss alone made his chest ache. He found some soup and fixings for tuna salad sandwiches. While the soup was heating up in the microwave, he kept his hands busy making the tuna. When she hadn't come down after he was finished, he went to the foot of the stairs and listened.

He could still hear the shower. Concern made him frown. He approached the door and knocked. "Grace? The food is ready. You almost finished?" He waited for her response, but there was only silence and the heavy spray of the water.

He turned the handle to find the door unlocked. Inside, her clothes were strewn on the floor in a haphazard fashion. His eyes traveled to the closed shower curtain. "Grace?"

When she didn't order him out, he knew something was wrong. Moving to the tub, he reached over and pushed the shower curtain aside. She leaned against the tile, her hands covered her face, and her shoulders shook with her silent weeping.

Emotion twisted his gut, thickened his throat. "Ah, sweetheart." Fully clothed, he stepped in and she turned to him, burying her face against his chest. He massaged her scalp, his other arm around her slender waist, holding her tightly to him as the water continued to drench them both.

In the wake of her cathartic tears, nothing stood between them at that moment. There was only a deep-seated need, only comfort.

Grace awakened slowly. She could smell a delicious coffee aroma that permeated her sleep and brought her up from the depths. Stretching, she felt a few twinges from the beating she'd received, her face tender to the touch.

For the first time in months, Sara's death didn't haunt her dreams. That was unexpected and wholly welcome.

"How did you sleep?"

Jordan's voice pushed her up from her prone position and her eyes tracked to the door. He leaned against the jamb bare-chested, looking more perfect than a man had any right to. The contours of his chest delineated by heavy muscle, sculpted shoulders and a flat abdomen that she couldn't seem to stop staring at.

It was evident that he hadn't heeded her protests that she was all right. That he could leave.

Instead, he'd wrapped those strong arms around her and bolstered her strength, which she had only held on to out of sheer stubbornness. She dropped her head, her hair a curtain covering her face. It didn't bother her that she'd broken down. It was a long time coming. What bothered her was that Jordan had seen it. She was sure he was thinking she wasn't fit to pursue this case to trial. That he would try to get her to quit the task force again.

"I didn't know you were still here." She brought the cup to her lips and sipped. "I can see you didn't listen to me last night when I told you to leave."

She lifted her head and pushed back her unruly hair. Taking a quick glance at the pillow beside her, she didn't see a telltale impression, but she could feel it in every part of her body. He'd slept beside her, holding her. She owed her peaceful slumber to the strength of his arms, which had kept the dreams at bay, the warmth of his body that had warded off the lingering ghosts.

The emotions that played around his irises made her stomach jump. "I stayed so you wouldn't be alone," he said softly. "It's not a crime to admit that you need comfort, Grace."

She'd spent the last two months totally and utterly alone with her guilt and her pain. She knew instinctively that Jordan could become someone she could care deeply about, already did. Walling herself off from this kind of entanglement was easier than giving everything that was inside you. When you lost that special someone, it was difficult to get pieces of yourself back. The loss of her friend Richard had overshadowed everything and the fact that she had to watch Sara die was even worse. She never wanted to feel that kind of pain again.

She wasn't sure she could let go of her fears completely. And she didn't know how to handle the effect his kindness and his gentleness had on her fractured heart, now in the process of being mended, slow bit by slow bit.

She got out of bed and when he got a full view of her face, he swore under his breath. He pushed off the jamb and was beside the bed in two long strides. Gently, he cupped her chin and she winced slightly. Not from the discomfort, but from the sheer heat of Jordan, that wonderful warmth that had chased away the ice in her limbs last night and calmed her raging nerves.

He turned her face so he could get a better look at her cheekbone. "Tell me your bruises look worse then they feel."

She reached up and covered his hand, her heart melting at the concern in his eyes and the care he took with her. She could have resisted him, she told herself, if he hadn't looked at her with such tenderness mingled with regret. She knew Jordan, and he was kicking himself for his part in her attack.

It seemed so natural to touch her lips to his. Her mouth moved on his, gently, sweetly. Moving nearer, she increased the pressure, the kiss full of wonder.

Jordan was drowning in sensation, battling a need that rose swiftly, was banked ruthlessly. He didn't want thanks and he damn well didn't want pity. A ragged sense of honor kept him motionless, when instinct dictated that he haul her into his arms. He vowed he would be careful with her, as if she was spun glass. Everything about her was beautiful to him.

Her mouth moved to his jaw, and he clenched it, hard, when her lips dragged over the stubble he hadn't shaved that morning. His lungs dragged in the scent of her in a guilty, greedy swallow, and his muscles quivered with the force of his control.

She didn't need this. The thought hammered in his head, keeping rhythm with the pulse in his veins. He didn't know what drove her, but he knew she was vulnerable in a way she'd never allowed herself to be before. Knew even her well-worn defenses must have limits.

"Grace, are you sure about what you want? Because I want to be clear here. I want you, now. No more pretenses."

"I'm sure, Jordan."

He was positive that in time her defenses would be firmly back in place. She was still reeling from her recent experiences. He tried to remember that as she caught his bottom lip between her teeth, scored it gently. Emotion he couldn't name twisted in his chest when she traced his mouth with the tip of her tongue. She needed time and distance to regroup.

Perhaps it would have been easier to withstand if this meant nothing to her but physical release. But there'd been emotion in her answer. And it was apparent in her kiss. Each touch crumbled his control a bit further.

Her fingers skimmed over his chest. His muscles jumped beneath her touch, quivering with an insatiable need. His hands went to her hips, thinking he should set her away from him, but unable to do it.

When her mouth returned to his, his arms snaked around her waist, and he kissed her back with a bruising passion that should have alarmed her. Should have had her pulling away. Instead, it enflamed them both.

His fingers glided through her mass of hair, cupping her scalp. He held her head still and devoured her mouth. And he imagined, just for a moment, what it would be like to make love to her without fearing the inevitable moment when her walls would go back up, locking him out and the memories away.

But there were no barriers between them now. The certainty shimmered between them, beckoned promisingly. And the knowledge was sweet, perhaps made more so because he knew how precious the moment was.

Her heart was racing, keeping pace with his. His tongue stabbed at her lips, and they parted in a seductive welcome. He brought her closer, one hand sweeping under her nightgown, smoothing over her silky back. She arched against him, and the last vestige of his control gave way under the weight of his need for her.

The freedom to touch her was a sinful pleasure, and best savored slowly. He reached for the hem of her nightgown, drew it over her head. Flesh pressed against flesh, and the sensation of her breasts flattened against his chest whipped his blood to a torrent. He skimmed his lips over the curve of her shoulder, his muscles tense, waiting for the rage of desire to subside again.

The bed was right behind him. He could ease her back just a matter of inches and they'd fall together, every inch of their bodies touching. They could give their passion free rein, forget all thoughts, all doubts. It would be easy and gloriously satisfying. He knew she'd welcome it, return it. Instead, he gave her more.

He bent to scoop her up in his arms and laid her on the bed. When he followed her down, it was with passion held in check, and something far more dangerous rising to the surface. He loomed half over her, combed her hair back from her bruised face with his fingers. An aching path of tenderness etched through him. It was an alarming emotion and gave him a momentary sense of fear at the power of it, but it was soon gone.

Her injuries had bloomed over the hours, ugly reminders of what she'd endured. His lips brushed over the bruise on her jaw and then found another beneath her eye.

In the bright sunlight from the open window, her skin was glossy pale, woman warm. Over the slope of her breasts, her nipples beckoned his mouth, the burgundy-rose buds hard and tempting. But then his eyes traveled up to her left shoulder where he could see the beginning of the damage the fire had done to her.

She felt his gaze and stilled, her eyes meeting his and he immediately felt her withdrawal. Her fear.

He touched her scar and she flinched. Such devastation the touch of fire could work. He couldn't stand it.

"It's so ugly," she whispered. "It'd be easier just not to look at it."

"No, Grace," he said softly, "Every inch of you is beautiful, so beautiful," he muttered, hurting for her.

Chapter 10

Grace felt the even pressure of his finger tracing her scar, all the way to its end. In time, the scar would flatten and thin out. Above her, the bones of his cheeks were hard.

"This?" He traced the scar again and said, "This is nothing but a badge of courage."

Grace remained perfectly still, uncertain of her response. He lowered his head and she felt his mouth move over her scarred shoulder. His gentleness undid her. Again he was offering her something she didn't know how to accept, or return. She only knew that the foreign experience tangled her emotions. Wreaked havoc on her system. The minutes stretched, lined with gold.

Jordan worked his way back up to her mouth, saw her eyes, glazed but wary. And comprehension slammed into him, so sudden and violent he was nearly bowled over by it. Defenses worked both ways. Walls were built as much to protect what was inside as to keep others out. He wondered if she knew which reason kept her so solid.

Their lips met, tongues entwined. The desire was still present, but contained for the moment. He gave her long stirring kisses; languid, lazy caresses. And when he felt her body melt against his, heard her breath hitch slightly, he knew this was what he wanted. What he'd always wanted. To feel her go pliant with pleasure. To feel her hands on his flesh. To know that with every gasp and moan he drew from her, she thought of him. Nothing but him.

His hands drifted over her breasts, fingers circling, never settling. Her breath hissed in and she reached for him, her fingers clutching his shoulders and skating over his chest. A thousand points of flame burst beneath his skin. Control wavered, took conscious effort to steady.

To pleasure her and himself, he dipped his head, drew her nipple into his mouth, savagely satisfied to hear his name tumble from her lips. Cupping her other breast in his hand, he fondled it until the dual assault had her body twisting against him.

A haze seemed to have formed over all thought, all reason. There was only Grace, her flavor tracing through his system, her scent embedded in his senses. Sunlight slanted through the window, a single ray painting their bodies. Her fingers were fumbling with his snap and zipper, and each slight brush of her knuckles against the front of his fly was the most exquisite form of torture.

Need streaked through him, made a mockery of his intentions. Easing away an inch, he helped her pull his pants down his legs and kicked them away. Then he rid them both of the only barrier left between them and pulled her to face him, until they lay together side by side so every inch of their bodies touched. Finding the pulse at the base of her throat, he laved it with his tongue. She drew up a leg, not quite innocently, let it glide over his hip.

His breath sawed out of his lungs. There was a reason to take it slow. But at the moment it was difficult to recall. His hand caressed the satin of her thigh, felt the whisper of muscle beneath the silky skin. It was always an erotic delight to rediscover Grace's softness. His fingers trailed closer to her core of heat, and he thrilled to her quiver.

She forgot to breathe. He gave her no choice but to feel. Grace gloried in the choice, even though she realized that it came with risk. But right now there was only his body close to hers, smooth flesh stretched over padded muscle. Her fingers traced over him, where sinew and bone joined to leave intriguing hollows. Each begged to be explored with soft lips and swift hands.

Longing battled with doubt. He drew his fingers along the crease where her leg met her hip and she stiffened, her lungs clogged. He was moving down her body, painting her flesh with his tongue. Her blood turned hot, molten, and chugged through her veins like lava. Her world, her focus, narrowed to include only the two of them.

Need, Jordan was finding, was a double-edged sword, one as painful as it was pleasurable. And, poised on that razor-edged peak, he was as primed as she was for a fall. He couldn't find it in himself to care. His mouth found her moist warmth and her back arched. He slipped his hands beneath her hips, lifted her to devour. The soft, strangled sounds tumbling from her lips urged him on, to take more. To give more. And when she shot to release in a wild shuddering mass, she cried his name.

Grace fought hard to haul breath into her lungs. Her limbs were weak, lax. And for the moment at least, she felt utterly tranquil. She felt the bed move, and her eyelids fluttered open. Tranquility abruptly fled. Here was the danger she'd forgotten, in the intensely masculine man bending over her. Her hand raised of its own volition, curved around his neck and brought his mouth to hers.

She'd never known desire to be quenched so completely, to return so quickly. He was hard, intriguingly so, and when her fingers went in exploration, he suffered her touch for only a moment before moving her hand away. Her lips curved. He was determined to maintain control. She was equally determined that he lose it.

She pushed him to his back, then went on a journey of discovery. His breath heaved out of his chest as her teeth scored his skin lightly, nipping a path from his shoulder to his belly. His restraint unraveled a bit more with each soft touch.

They rolled across the sheets, into and out of the sunlight spilling onto the bed. Jordan's gentleness had vanished, hunger raging. His vision misted, but his other senses were hyperalert. Achingly so. The sweet, dark flavor of her tongue battling with his. The silkiness of her curly hair brushing against his skin and the sexy, tight grasp of her hands as she explored him where he was hot, hard and pulsing.

The teasing was gone. Gentleness was beyond him. His arousal was primal, basic and immediate. His hands battled hers, and he rolled her to his side, drew her leg over his hip. Testing her readiness with one finger, he watched her eyelids droop.

"Look at me, Grace," he demanded, his voice as ragged as his control. "Open your eyes."

He moved into position, quickly using protection, his shaft barely parting her warm cleft, and stilled. Only when she dragged her eyelids open, eyes dazed and unfocused, did he ease into her, pausing as she twisted and moaned against him. He moved in tiny increments, not satisfied until he was seated deep inside her. Then he took her mouth with his own, savagely aware that they were touching, every inch of their bodies. Inside and out. And still it wasn't enough.

He withdrew from her only to lunge again, each time deeper, harder, faster. They were caught in a vortex, spinning wilder and wilder. Out of control. He saw her face spasm, felt the clench of her inner muscles, swallowed her cry with his mouth. And then, only then, did he let the tide sweep him under and dash him up and over the edge.

Minutes, or hours, later he stroked a hand along the curve of her waist before settling it passively on her hip. Each beat of her heart was echoed with his. Their breathing slowed, and eventually reason intruded. He started to move away, and her fingers tightened in an automatic reflexive response. Reluctantly, he ignored it. He took care of it and rolled back to her. To please himself, he pushed the heavy curls away from her face, and skimmed his fingertips over her shoulder and down her arm.

Then he sank down with her, into the softness of her, and curled around her as they simply let themselves be.

Among some of the most intimate moments in life was waking up next to a man. To compound it, Jordan had elicited emotions, wants and needs inside Grace that had been released. She wasn't sure how she was going to contain them all, get them back under her control. She watched him in sleep, the rise and fall of his wide chest, the way his dark hair framed his face, the thickness of his eyelashes dusting his cheeks.

No matter how much she'd avoided this moment with him, here she was. Tension carved crazy eights into her stomach. In the past she'd taken such care to avoid just this moment. But now that it was upon her, she would have to find some way to simplify her relationship with Jordan.

Right, she thought with a jeer at herself.

The man beside her had been nothing but a complication since they met.

Her work sustained her, and the fact that she was a control freak. She saw that clearly. Her friendship with Sara was the one sustaining relationship in her life. She'd relied on Sara—they were so close. When Sara died, and Grace was unable to prevent her from dying, it shook her very foundations, took away her sense of control and left her untethered and floating in uncertain waters.

Jordan twisted in his sleep, jerking. He made a guttural noise and turned, his body restless and tense. Caught up in the nightmare, he called out. "Dan, don't do it!"

"Jordan," she said softly, touching his shoulder. He cried out in anguish, his face contorted in unspeakable agony. "Jordan," she said louder and shook him, alarmed.

His eyes popped open and he gazed at her for a moment. "What? What's wrong?"

"You were having a nightmare, I think. It was a bad one."

"Damn," he sat up, rubbing sleep out of his eyes. "Unfortunately, it's not just a nightmare, Grace."

"Oh," she said, finally giving in to her curiosity about Jordan. "Who is Dan? Is he the reason you left the FBI?"

"Yes."

"What happened? Tell me about it."

He shifted away from her, but she moved closer. "Jordan, you're the one who said we needed to go deeper with our feelings, remember?"

"Yes, I did." He took a deep breath and let it out. "I was a hostage negotiator. Had an almost perfect record. I worked too much, drank too much to mask the stress it caused to have lives in my hands. I think you know what I mean."

Grace scooted closer to him, wrapped her arms around his chest and snuggled close. "I do know that feeling. I've imbibed a few times to release stress myself."

"It makes it all the more difficult to take, Grace. Dan Matthews was my best friend, just as Sara was yours. I worked next to him every day and I didn't see the signs. I was trained for it, but in him I just dismissed it as the kind of cynicism that gets to all of us after a while."

"Tell me," she said. "I won't judge you. God forbid. You haven't judged me."

"I did, a bit, at first, but then I got to know you and realized that you were just as human as we all are."

"Yeah, try as I might, bullets don't bounce off my chest."

He smiled and toyed with her hair. "One day he came into the office. He pulled out his gun and opened fire. Killed three agents before I brought him down. He shot me in the shoulder and we sat across from each other."

"That's why you have this scar here," she said, gently moving her fingers over it.

He nodded, and then continued. "I tried to negotiate. He told me we couldn't make a difference no matter how we tried. It was better to put these people out of their misery now. He pointed the gun at me, but I guess at the last minute he decided to let me live. He turned the gun on himself."

Grace tightened her arms around him. The story was so similar to hers, but with such an ugly twist. He couldn't save his friend, and she'd been unable to save Sara. Sara had died quietly and Dan hadn't, yet they both had died so quickly, leaving their best friends traumatized.

"I tried to forgive myself. It's been two years since that happened and I still have nightmares about it. Even in my dream I can't save him."

"So when you told me you understood my guilt, you really did. We're both survivors."

"Are we? Or are we simply the walking wounded?"

"You've managed to change your career, and as far as I can see, you're functioning normally. Maybe you should take your own advice and give yourself a break."

"I will when you do."

"Ha! Blackmail." She sobered. "I'm sorry, Jordan."

"So am I. He was a good man and a good agent. I miss him."

"I miss Sara, too. So much."

Unbidden, the feelings of guilt rose up in her and for the first time since she'd lost Sara, they weren't as strong, or as poignant. She had Jordan to thank for that. His presence eased some of the ache.

"How about we get something to eat? I'm starving."

"It's good to hear you say that."

"Good. You can make me breakfast. Coffee, too, with plenty of cream."

"Can do on the food, but the coffee and cream… um…I'm afraid you're out."

"Oh, no. That's a tragedy."

"Never fear. I have a car and some money. I will go out and pick them up. Be back in a jif."

She laughed. "Great, and thank you. Hey, do you think you could take me over to the car dealership today? I really need to buy a car."

"I can. Then we should go in and see what's happening with our case."

She nodded. "I want to be there when they arraign him. I want to see every step they take to make him pay for what he's done."

Jordan got dressed and Grace couldn't put into words how sorry she was that he was putting clothing on that fabulous body of his.

When he left, she dragged all her dirty clothes down the stairs and proceeded to start her laundry. She went out onto the deck and checked her bird feeder.

She jumped when she heard a twig snap, her head jerking around at the sound. She peered into the woods that bracketed her property, the murkiness deep even with the bright sunshine. She got a sudden chill, as if someone was watching her. She stepped back, the feeder forgotten. Then out of the gloom scampered a squirrel. It chittered at her before bounding off, flicking its tail as it went. Jim Lyons was in jail and she had nothing to fear anymore.

She laughed, releasing the tension in her shoulders.

She walked to her shed, pulled out her ladder and set it against the tree. Climbing, she finished with that feeder, too, and went back into the house.

Upstairs in her room, she made the bed then stripped down and got into the shower. When Jordan came back, they would have a leisurely breakfast, then maybe she could entice him back upstairs...

Had that been a floorboard creaking? She shut off the faucet and got out of the shower. Drying off quickly, she put on her robe, feeling oddly exposed. She opened the bathroom door.

"Jordan?"

There was no answer and her tight stomach got tighter. She came out of the bathroom into her bedroom and stopped dead. A camera sat on a tripod so it could take photos of the whole room.

Grace cried out and looked around, but there was no one there. She made a beeline for her bedroom door when her house shook from two explosions.

The sound of the blast was loud in the stillness. It boomed across the woods, setting birds into flight.

Grace smelled smoke and she frantically pulled at the door, but it wouldn't budge. She was trapped inside her bedroom!

Panic twisted inside her like a live thing, and she backed up against the wall, staring at the door. She slid down the wall, closing her eyes against the fear that strummed through her blood, made her heart pound.

She buried her face against her knees and trembled. All her training abandoned her, all her control smashed.

She heard a faint ringing and realized that it was her cell phone. She'd brought her purse upstairs with her last night.

She scrambled for her purse, searching frantically for her cell. When she got it, she that saw it was Jordan calling.

"My house is on fire. Jordan, help me, please," she yelled into the phone. Her hand gripped the phone and it was all she could do not to give in to blind panic again. "I'm trapped!"

Chapter 11

"What the hell happened?" Jordan's shout reverberated through the phone.

"I don't know. Someone was in the house. There's a camera on a tripod in my room. There were explosions."

"Son of a bitch! Are you all right?"

"Yes, I'm unharmed for now, but there's a lot of smoke. I'm in the bedroom and I know how to stem the smoke coming in. It will slow it a little bit. But there's no way out."

"Did you call the fire department?"

"No."

"Call 911. I'm almost there."

Grace hung up, dialed 911 and reported the fire. She coughed as smoke started wafting under the door. It was completely foreign to her to be experiencing a fire as a victim. Running to the bathroom, she pulled a towel off the rack and rolled it up, her hands shaking. She ran to the door and shoved it against the crack between the bottom of the door and the floor. It stemmed some of the flow of smoke. She got another towel and threw it over the camera. Quickly, she ran to her closet and pulled out jeans and a T-shirt. With her heart pounding, she got dressed.

Then she retreated to the corner of her bedroom. Opening the window for ventilation, she slid down the wall. This time she was all alone.

No, that wasn't true. She wasn't alone in this. She had Jordan. He was coming. He'd promised to protect her.

She lay down to take advantage of the cleaner air as the room filled with smoke. A breeze from the window helped to keep fresh oxygen in the room.

She heard sirens in the background and thought halfheartedly that everyone was going to be too late. Just as she was with Sara.

Then she heard it—something hit hard against the house. She got up and ran over to the window. Outside she saw Jordan climbing up the ladder she used to fill her bird feeder.

"Grace!" he said, coming in through the window, an axe gripped in one fist.

He pulled her into his arms. He cupped her cheek. His eyes searched her face, no doubt reading her fear.

"I'm here. We'll be okay. The fire department is right behind me."

Something scraped against the house and they both froze. When Grace peered out the window her stomach lurched. "Oh, God. The ladder."

Jordan crowded near her. "Son of a bitch. I swear when I catch this bastard, I'm going to strangle him with my bare hands. We'll have to wait for the fire department. It shouldn't be long."

"Just another fun-filled day with Grace."

"Sweetheart, when this is all over, I'll show you what real fun is."

"You promise?"

"I haven't let you down so far, have I?"

She looked up at him, her eyes meeting his squarely. "No," she said fiercely, grabbing at the lapels of the overalls. "No, you haven't."

The sirens grew louder by the second. She could hear the powerful engines grinding up the steep incline of the road outside her house.

Her cell rang—a small but reassuring noise penetrating the din coming from outside. It was Mike. "Grace what is your location?"

"The bedroom. It faces out the back. First window to the right."

Instantly, he was shouting orders to the others, even as he tried to reassure Grace. She could hear his voice through the open window now as well as the phone. "Get the ladder to the back of the house! First window on the right. Move it, double time! Hang on, kid, we're coming. Manning, pull that hose and get it hooked. Start the flow. Let's go!"

Jordan rose and dragged her up with him. He leaned out of the window. "Watch out below!" He put his hand out and pushed her back slightly. "Stand back," he said as he gripped the axe in both hands, his forearms and back bunching with powerful muscle. He swung the axe and knocked out the window, glass and wood shattered. With his gloved hands, he pushed out the remaining glass to make it safer for them to climb over the sill.

A ladder hit the side of the house and Dave Sanders

appeared at the window. "Let's get you two out of there."

"Take Grace first." Flames were beginning to lick at the doorjamb to her room, thick, choking smoke billowed into the room from the encroaching fire.

She looked down to make sure it was safe and dropped her purse out the window. Then she stepped onto the ladder with practiced ease. She'd done this with sixty pounds of gear on, so doing it now in jeans and a T-shirt and bare feet was a breeze. And it felt good to let her training and experience kick in finally.

She climbed down as fast as she could, Jordan coming behind her, albeit a little slower.

When he touched down on the ground, they moved away from the house to the front where Smitty waited. He slipped oxygen masks over each of their faces and forced them to sit down. She drew in the potent air and sighed as her breathing eased.

They couldn't speak, but Jordan communicated with eye contact. Then he took her hand, clasping it in his own, saying with his eyes how relieved he was that she was unharmed.

When Smitty was satisfied that they'd had enough oxygen, he removed the masks. "You two take it easy. Smoke inhalation is nothing to fool around with. You should know that, Grace. Make sure he does."

She nodded. "It's mild, Smitty. We weren't exposed for that long and we had an open window to provide oxygen."

"Good. You know, I do miss you around the station, but we've got to stop meeting like this."

She laughed and nodded. "Agreed."

"Take care." With a parting, reassuring smile, Smitty walked away toward the front of the truck. The firefighters of her station were still working on the fire, but Grace held out no hope of saving her house.

Most of her neighbors were at work, but the ones who were home clustered at the edge of the road, watching all the activity, their faces wreathed with concern.

Jordan rose, then crouched down on his haunches, bringing his face closer to eye level. In the brightness of the day, his eyes were starkly blue. "That is something I don't want to go through ever again. I could have lost you."

She coughed and cleared her thick throat. "If it wasn't for you, I'm not sure I would have made it out of there alive. I'm a firefighter, for God's sake, and I fell apart like an amateur. I don't know what is wrong with me."

"Maybe you're not quite ready to talk about it."

"Seems somehow that I'm sticking my head in the sand."

He stood and reached his hand down to her. "Come on."

She stayed put. "Is that an order?"

"Not an order, a request. Sitting here feeling sorry for ourselves isn't going to help us catch this bastard. Let's get back to work and decide where to focus our energy."

Energy. It emanated off him in waves without him even trying. His speaking voice was low, calm, smooth. Only the tic in his jaw, the gleam in his eyes gave away his agitation at the moment.

"What makes you think I won't make another mistake? Maybe I should do as you say and quit the task force."

"We both got duped by the arsonist, Grace, so we're both to blame. We were being led around by the nose.

That pisses me off. That should piss you off, too. So, you see? You can't quit. If you do, he wins." He reached his hand down again. "Don't let that happen. We're a team."

She hadn't wanted this, but there was nothing she could do about it now. She had it. The only good part about any of this was that Jordan wouldn't be leaving. It wasn't until just now that she realized how badly she wanted him to stay. Maybe she did want to hide her head in the sand and not admit to herself or anyone else what was really the crux of the problem. But maybe she needed the impetus to jolt her into action.

Or maybe she just didn't want him to leave because she wasn't done figuring out what she wanted to do about him yet.

She could have stood on her own, but something made her deliberately take his offer. She reached her hand up to his. The contact was every bit as electric as she'd known it would be. His palm was wide and warm, his grip steady and strong as he tugged her easily to her feet. But rather than let her go as she'd expected, he kept tugging, until she stumbled a step closer and came up flush against his body. His free arm was instantly around her back, steadying her, keeping her tucked up against him.

"I'm not playing games," he told her, the intensity of his gaze impossible to look away from at such close range. "You're still in trouble here, Grace. I expect you to stick close to me."

She was in trouble, all right. Deep, heart-thumping trouble. She opened her mouth to speak, but nothing came out. It had been a very long time since there was anyone in her life who cared where she was or what she did. Much less if she was safe or even alive.

She'd be lying if she said she didn't like the feeling of being looked after, for the moment anyway. "I took care of myself just fine, until you came along." Her voice wobbled dangerously. He didn't have to know it was more because of him than from the threat of some unseen enemy.

"So did I."

"What is that supposed to mean?"

"It means—" He broke off, his gaze making its own telltale slip down to her mouth, then back up again. "I don't usually worry this much about someone I'm guarding."

"You don't need to worry about me."

"I may not need to, but I do. Just do me a favor and stick close, as I said."

"Well, right now, I couldn't be any closer."

Rather than set her free, his arm flexed against her back, drawing her more tightly, making her gasp as she came up against the full, hard length of him. Harder in some places than others. "From now on, we stick together until we're sure this is over."

She tried to smile, tried to find some way to make light of a situation that was rapidly becoming anything but. "It might be a bit difficult to walk around joined at the hip."

He pulled her hand up to his chest, pressed it there before letting it go so he could slide his fingers beneath the hair at her nape and tug her mouth closer to his. And she didn't do a damn thing to stop him. "You made me crazy when I first met you, and you're making me crazy now. I have no defenses."

"Is that bad?" she asked, her voice barely more than a whisper against her suddenly constricted throat.

"Is what bad?" he said, getting lost in her eyes.

She laughed. "I asked if it was a bad thing that you have no defenses."

"I don't know. I can't think straight." He brushed a strand of hair off her forehead, and when he spoke, his tone was gentler, completely undoing her.

"Just…stick close. Okay?"

His mouth dropped onto hers as simple and as easy as breathing. Everything was tangled up in her head and in her heart. She didn't even try to convince herself that she knew the difference anymore.

A cold voice behind them said, "The firefighter becomes the victim again. Or does she?"

She jerked away from Jordan and turned to see Tom Parker standing a short distance away, surveying them. "It's good to see that you survived the fire." His words seemed nothing more than platitudes when she considered the look of hate in his eyes.

She glared at him. "Tom…what are you doing here?"

"I heard about the fire on my radio."

And, of course, he had to come, Grace thought with irritation. Why was it that since Sara's death, Tom had always been nearby to witness every catastrophe that befell her? Each disastrous event seemed like a magnet, pulling him to her again and again. Any sympathy she might have felt for Tom had vanished long ago under the onslaught of his seemingly continual presence, reveling in her pain.

"How is it that you always seem to be nearby when something bad happens to me?"

Tom looked at Jordan, then back at her. There was something menacing in his eyes. Was he jealous that she had found something with Jordan and he had lost his wife? Angry to see that something good might actually be happening to her?

He shrugged. "I'm a police officer. Someone's got to get on this problem," he replied. "So far, no one seems to know how to handle a simple investigation. No one seems to be able to figure out who killed my wife."

Grace felt Jordan bristle at the implied accusation. "While I'm here, I'll question your neighbors. Maybe they saw something that can help."

Grace watched him walk away, and this time she couldn't let it go. His body language told her he was angry. She guessed that it was because he'd lost Sara. The pain of that loss was foreign to her before Jordan. Now she couldn't imagine how Tom was able to handle the agony of losing someone he loved.

She extricated herself from Jordan's arms and ran after Tom. "You blame me, don't you?"

Tom turned on her, his eyes narrowed and fierce. "Every day, Grace, when I wake up, Sara isn't there. But you wake up every day and live your life. Why couldn't it have been you instead of her?"

"Why hide your feelings, Tom? It's best to get them out in the open."

He stabbed a finger at her. "Every time I look at you, it's a reminder that Sara is dead. Are those the feelings you're talking about? I think we're clear here about how I *feel*."

Her sense of discomfort whenever she was around Tom returned tenfold. He *was* angry at her and hadn't forgiven her. Her guilt swelled inside her like a choking disease. In the past it seemed as if Tom was jabbing at her with reminders of his loss. He always seemed to be around where she was. Was that a coincidence?

And what exactly did that mean?

Did Tom want to do her harm?

Worried by Tom's words and his sense of weird timing, she headed toward her smoldering house. Jordan followed her, close on her heels.

"What was that about, Grace?"

"Tom blames me for Sara's death. I had a feeling he did, and it's justified in his mind. I got the sense of his seething anger at her funeral. Body language is always truer than words."

"Do you think he's a threat?"

"I don't know. He's a police officer, and plenty of them have snapped and done terrible things."

"It might be a good idea to question him about his whereabouts during the times you've been threatened."

"Let's do that covertly. I wouldn't want to be responsible for exposing him to accusations that are unfounded. He's been through a lot and although he blames me, I understand his pain. I loved Sara, too."

Jordan nodded.

Coughing, she lifted her hand to her face to cover her mouth. Her heart tightened even further in her chest as she surveyed the damage. The exterior walls were charred by black soot. When she rounded the back, she saw that the roof was half-gone, and the windows had all blown out and were scorched. From what she could tell, the interior looked completely ravaged.

Which meant the whole thing would have to come down and be rebuilt.

The longer she stared at the charred remains, the angrier she got. The heightened emotions of the past few days, coupled with the rage building inside her at this latest violation of her property, all fused together in that moment to form one huge outburst of fury. "Who is doing this to me? I'm not going to rest until I figure out who the hell is doing this. I swear!"

Jordan wrapped his arms around her and she reached up to wipe the tears from her face. At the moment, the anger felt good, energizing, as though she was finally coming out of a long daze and taking action. "I'm so royally pissed."

"That's good. Just don't let it make you do anything stupid."

She was rigid for a moment before the fight streamed out of her and she allowed herself to lean against him. For just a moment. It wasn't that difficult, she discovered, to lean on a strong shoulder if she tried hard enough.

Mike came over. "I'm sorry about your house, Grace. So sorry about all this. How are you holding up?"

"I'm doing okay, Mike, thanks."

"I suppose you two want to get in there?"

"We do," Jordan said.

"Well, you're going to have to give my boys some time before you investigate. We've got to knock this fire down and make sure it stays out. How about later on today? I'll give you a call."

Jordan and Grace left her ruined home and headed down into the city. At a convenience store, Jordan bought her some flip-flops so she'd have something to wear on her feet. She was thankful she had kept her purse with her. At least she had access to her money.

"I'll need some things. Could we go by the mall?"

"Sure."

"So it looks like Lyons may be off the hook," Grace said.

"Looks like it, but we shouldn't let him go until we check out your house and see how the fire started. Although I'm pretty certain what we'll find."

"The evidence we had against Jim was damning."

"But it seemed too easy. Too pat. We should have stayed on our guard," Jordan said.

"We didn't have any reason to think that anyone else was involved. We certainly didn't believe he was framed. All suspects say that."

"Vulcan tried to make you 'one with the fire' again," Jordan said.

"Yes, and if he framed Jim, then he has contacts in the police or fire departments because there was no one around except police and firefighters when I talked about Richard's notes."

"So that makes you think we were overheard?"

"Yes, unless he followed me and just used Richard's notes as an excuse to knock me around and place the blame on Lyons."

"That's certainly a possibility." He slowed and turned into the vast parking lot of the shopping mall.

Grace leaned back into her seat. "He must have taken the opportunity to grab Richard's notes and plant them in Jim's garage."

Jordan pulled into a parking space and cut the engine. "I understand your hesitation. He's been methodical up until now."

Grace shook her head. "Not really. I always felt the fire that killed Richard and Sara was somehow different."

He glanced at her eyebrows raised. "Rushed?" he suggested.

Grace released her seat belt. "Yes, as if he didn't have the time he needed to plan it out fully."

"It was effective, though."

Grace stared at the flat building in front of her, not looking forward to the crowds. She turned to Jordan.

"Yes, if Richard was the target, it was very effective. But why take the pictures? What was that about?"

Jordan shrugged. "Maybe he wanted to relive the experience. Serial arsonists—especially those who target homes the way he did—are just plain serial killers in my book. It's the thrill of the fire and the thrill of the kill that drives them. Maybe he wanted to savor the moment over and over again."

"As serial killers do when they take something from the victim? A way to get back the memory of what it felt like to kill?" Grace shivered, unable to believe that they may have discovered that the person who was trying to murder her was, in fact, a serial killer. She needed to get back to the office to do some research.

Grace reached to open the car door, but Jordan slipped his hand over hers. "Grace, I'm sorry about your house. Sorry that you lost everything."

She looked at their entwined hands. "You saved what was most important, Jordan. Things can be replaced."

He nodded and pulled her tightly into his arms, holding her for a moment. When he let her go, they got out of the vehicle and entered the mall.

An hour and forty-five minutes later, they were back at Jordan's hotel, booking Grace in the room next to his once again. Luckily, it hadn't been taken.

Grace put away her new belongings, including the suitcase and garment bag she'd purchased to hold everything.

She donned a pair of tan slacks, but hesitated over the shirt. While purchasing several practical button-down shirts, she had impulsively bought a pretty, white, sleeveless blouse made out of eyelet lace. The material wouldn't cover all her scars. They would be exposed.

She debated for a moment, and with her stomach tight, she chose the white eyelet blouse. Pulling her hair back from her bruised face, she secured it into a ponytail. The bruises on her face were stark and multicolored.

Instead of seeing them as something to be ashamed of, she chose to see them as a badge of courage, just as Jordan had said. She'd been fighting for justice when she'd gotten them. She would be proud of that.

When she came out of the bathroom, Jordan was waiting for her. He was dressed in a beautiful blue pin-striped suit with a silk tie in variegated blues. His dark hair was combed, but it still gave him a dangerous edge. He'd shaved the stubble from his face.

"You look very…spiffy."

"Spiffy?" he said, making a face.

"Okay, powerful and sexy."

"Mmm, I like that much better."

He eyed her blouse, but didn't say anything. He didn't have to. She could see the approval on his face and for the first time since she'd been injured, it actually felt good to be alive. She also felt way too good about Jordan's approval, but she wasn't going to examine that feeling too closely.

The task force office was empty when they arrived. Grace wasted no time. She headed for her computer and turned it on. The box of Richard's notes sat near her desk. She pulled off the top and rummaged through them while her computer booted up.

Not far from the top, she found Richard's datebook. She opened it to the day he died. She was surprised to find Sara's name penned in at two o'clock.

Richard had an appointment with Sara the day he died? Why? What did he want to talk to her about? And what was it Sara wanted to talk to Grace about that same day? She realized that these had to be connected. Sara and Grace had a tight bond. Sara told her everything.

She went through more of Richard's notes going back a week before his death.

> I'm beginning to think there's a pattern to these fires that have been plaguing La Rosa. It's interesting to discover that the MO of the arsonist I have been tracking for some time seems to have developed over time. A learn-as-you-go method. Six people have already died, and I'm determined to find the killer. I'm half-convinced that is what he is. A killer. A serial killer.
>
> I have a suspicion of who the arsonist is. I made the connection purely by accident. I noticed a dry spell of about five years between the last fires and the new ones that are being set. There is often a significant change in an arsonist's life that can cause this type of behavior. I'm just sorry if it is the person I suspect—the revelation will have a profound and detrimental effect on someone I hold in great esteem.

Grace set down the notes and picked up two folders labeled, *Previous Arsons: MO Coke Can* and *Recent Arsons: MO Coke Can and Green Lighter.*

She opened the folder to find that Richard had cataloged all the fires in La Rosa that were remotely connected to the MO. Grace was astonished to discover that there were so many. Richard had found a connection between them.

She settled back and pulled out all of Richard's files.

There was a thick file full of crime scene photos.

Arson investigators took numerous photos of all crime scenes because most arsonists enjoyed watching their handiwork. The arsonists were often caught in photos and then apprehended.

It was a lot of material to go over, but she was determined to go through it all very carefully.

"Jordan, Richard had a suspicion about who the arsonist was."

Jordan came over to her. "He didn't say in his notes who he suspected?"

"No, just that he had a suspicion. And get this—Sara had an appointment with him the day he died."

"No kidding. What do you think it was about?"

"I don't know. They could have been having a late lunch for all I know. Sara's dad was a fly fisherman and Richard loved fishing. Sara inherited her father's love of tying flies. They had that in common."

"Looks like we've got a long day ahead of us. I'm going to put on a pot of coffee."

"Sounds like a good idea."

They each worked steadily through Richard's files and made notes about anything that they found important.

At around ten o'clock, Grace put down a file and leaned back, rubbing her eyes.

"I think it's about time to call it quits for today," Jordan said.

She nodded.

They closed up the office and once inside the SUV, Jordan asked, "Where do you want to eat?" They decided to go to the drive-through of a late-night burger joint for food.

Grace was munching on fries as they drove toward their hotel when she caught a glimpse of smoke, then she smelled it.

190

"Jordan…"

"I see it!" he said, turning sharply and heading for the smoke. When they got closer, Grace could see the flames licking at the front door to a very posh house.

"Oh, my God," Jordan said.

"Isn't that the mayor's mansion?" Grace said, her heart pounding in her chest as Jordan stopped out front and exited the vehicle without hesitation.

Chapter 12

Fire geysered up, licking at the eaves, setting a nearby tree on fire. The flames were golden and orange, curling and deadly in their beauty.

And Grace sat there watching it while Jordan kicked in the front door and disappeared inside. She sat there in a daze and faced her deadliest fear.

She was afraid of fire.

She wasn't going to get past it.

With a concerted effort, she reached for her cell phone and dialed 911, reporting the fire and giving the address. Shortly after that she heard the sirens.

But she didn't move, even as shame squirmed inside her, even as she knew Jordan could have perished, the mayor and his family could have died.

The image of Sara's face, her terrified eyes and her struggling fight to draw breath only brought back

Grace's remembered pain of gasping for each breath, the searing agony of the fire's touch.

And she was afraid.

So very afraid.

She felt unfit and like such a failure, and she didn't know how she was going to face Jordan. She was a firefighter and her training, even her instincts, failed her.

Jordan came out of the house. He was covered in soot, clutching a small child and firmly holding on to a sobbing woman who had to be Greg's wife. Greg came out behind him, carrying an even smaller child and Grace's heart squeezed in her chest at her inability to help them. She felt powerless and frustrated. She wanted to do something, anything, to help. She managed to get out of the SUV, but the heat of the fire reached out and slapped at her, pushed her back.

An EMT pulled up, and Jordan headed directly for the truck. He'd barely recovered from one bout of smoke inhalation and now he was dealing with another.

The arsonist was escalating. He must be aware that she had escaped the fiery death he'd planned for her. One he hoped to catch on a closed-circuit camera.

She watched as firefighters rushed toward the blaze and she envied them their stoic courage as they pulled on their masks and took up their hoses.

Even in her abject misery, she was so proud to have been a firefighter. She mourned the loss of something vital to her.

Jordan searched for her and when his eyes found her, she could see that he was concerned. Coward that she was, she turned away and walked right into Tom Parker.

Grace started to apologize, but Tom's scathing look made the words die on her lips.

"Well, well, Grace. It seems Jordan is the only one who has the presence of mind to handle himself with a sense of purpose. You, on the other hand, choked. What's the matter? Lost your nerve?"

There was no pretense on his part. In fact, he looked almost maniacal with the flames burning in his eyes, smoke wafting across them when the wind changed.

"It's no wonder Sara died. You were powerless to help her when she needed you and you're powerless now."

Jordan put a hand on Tom's chest and made him take a step back. "Listen, Parker. Why don't you go do your damn job and get off Grace's case? You don't know a damn thing about her, so don't pretend you do. Now get out of here."

Tom gave Grace another sneering look and stalked off.

"That guy really has some issues," Jordan said. "All this time he was masking a seething contempt for you. It might be best to steer clear of him."

Grace faced Jordan. She saw the angry welt on his wrist and another one on the side of his neck. "You're burned," she said, touching his arm.

"I'm fine. They're superficial."

"And the mayor and his family?"

"Kelly!" Greg stalked over and grabbed Jordan by the shoulder and spun him around. "I want this bastard found. Do you understand me? He almost killed me and my family!"

"Yes, Greg. I understand."

"Find him, Jordan," Greg said, his voice breaking as he looked over at his family. He turned and walked away, gathering his wife and kids against him as they huddled together in a small mass of solidarity.

"Let's go back to the hotel so I can get cleaned up," Jordan said.

They said nothing as he drove. Once back at the hotel, Grace stayed close to him until he headed for the shower. She wanted a run, but knew that wasn't going to happen. She couldn't sit still so she paced the room, knowing what she had to do. Knowing it was the right thing to do.

Jordan emerged from the shower with nothing but a towel around his waist.

Her entire body responded to his nearness. She needed to tell him what was on her mind, but she got scared, scared she would see disappointment, even contempt in his eyes.

"I need to talk to you," she said.

"All right."

She twisted her hands together. When Jordan saw her agitation, he moved closer. His first instinct was always to comfort her. She felt tenderness swell inside her for this man.

He covered her hands with his. "Grace, you can tell me anything."

She felt tears prick the back of her eyes. She wrapped her arms around his neck and held on to him.

"Anything," he murmured.

She should be talking, but instead she found his willing mouth. He accepted her tongue with a smooth ease that melted her bones. But what started as a simple kiss quickly turned into something else entirely. She'd thought she was keeping it together, that she was handling this, but it turned out that she was far from in control of the emotions he'd stirred inside her.

She kissed him as she'd never kissed a man in her life. She poured everything she had into it. Every single confusing, exhilarating, profoundly life-changing thing he'd ever made her feel was shoved right on out there. Let him deal with it—he'd provoked it, after all.

Not that he was complaining.

Her hands moved from his face to his hair, then rapidly down to his shoulders, where she tightened her grip so she could kiss him even more deeply. Her heart was pounding so hard she could hear the thrum of it in her ears, and it was quite probable that the moaning sounds echoing in the room were all coming from her. She didn't care. She reached down and loosened the towel, cupping his heavy arousal in her hand. She pulled at her blouse with the other and he helped to get her free of the clothes that were nothing more than a barrier. She was wild to feel his skin again, to sink into the blissful, mind-blowing place where she didn't have to worry about her conscience, her guilt, her fears. She wanted to drown herself in the knowledge that he could very easily—oh, so easily—take her to another place, a place where it was about nothing more than sensation, feeling, pleasure.

Her fingers fumbled at the button of her pants and, suddenly frustrated and completely out of patience, she pulled at them.

"Whoa," he said, covering her hands and trying to disengage his mouth from hers. When she kept on clawing at the button, he stilled her hands.

"Hang on," he said and reached down and flipped it open in one smooth move. "What's gotten into you?"

"You. You've gotten into me. And I don't know how to handle it. My whole world is turning upside down and I can't make any sense of it anymore. I'm feeling things

I have no business feeling about a man I just met. I'm confused as hell, scared as hell, and I don't know what to do about it."

Gently he cupped her face with his hands. "You trust me. And trust this." He leaned in and kissed her, only this kiss wasn't an assault on her senses…it was a promise. When he lifted his head, he kept his face close to hers. Their gazes locked. "I know it's crazy. Insane, even. But so what? I'm right where I want to be. You?"

She could only nod.

With practiced ease, he ran her zipper down and pushed her pants off her hips. The sheer masculine presence of him made her completely breathless, his hands gliding over her body like silk.

The air was still, the scent of him lingered around her, invisible and provocative, a clean, masculine smell.

Jordan was breathless with the feel of her skin beneath his palms. It was different from the other time they had made love, more thoughtful and yet familiar. Not just in the raging need he always had for her, but…it was Grace. She should feel new to him, a stranger, and yet he knew her, knew her in a way he'd never known anyone else. No walls, no guarded moments, no worrying about where it might lead. It had already led.

Yes, she was known to him, in that soul-deep way where like recognized like, mate recognized mate. It should have terrified him, right down to his core. And, he supposed, if he let it, it would. But she was Grace. And she was his. And there was nothing terrifying in that; there was only joy. Life wasn't fair. He knew that better than anyone, both from personal endurance and intimate observation. There was never a promise of time, and anyone who thought otherwise was a fool.

He liked to think he was no fool.

Even if he could stay here forever, there were no guarantees on what he and Grace might have, or for how long. Plans could be made, but life, or fate, often had something else in mind. His time, their time was now. He'd take the now and worry about the later, later.

He kissed her along the side of her jaw, down along her neck, across her collarbone. She sighed, tipped her head back and moaned softly as he indulged in a slow exploration that trailed around her breasts, with brief stops to pay particular attention to her engorged and deliciously erect nipples, before slipping lower. But when he reached her hipbone, she tugged him back and began an exploration of her own.

"Give me a chance," she said softly, making him wish he had something to hold on to as she made his knees weaken with her own lingering trail of kisses. When she reached his hip, he tugged her down on the bed, but she pushed him onto his back and went right back to exploring. "Just let me," she said, then returned to the mission at hand. Or at mouth, as the case may be.

He was going to object, going to pull her up on top of him, glide inside her and make love to her as slowly, as sweetly as he was capable of, but then he was groaning and arching off the bed as she took him into the delightfully warm and soft interior of her mouth. Her hands pushed at his chest, kept him in place as she slid her leg over his, making her intentions clear. And far be it from him to withhold from her what she wanted. Especially when—

"Sweet damn," he said followed by a long slow growl as she began moving her mouth and hand on him. "Grace, that's—" But there were no words. So he groped for a pillow, pulled it under his head and watched and felt and pumped his hips, as she brought him screamingly close to the edge.

And she would have taken him over, but not this time, not tonight. He nudged her away. "Come here," he murmured, helping her adjust her weight over him, then slowly easing her down onto him. Their sighs of pleasure matched. "You're so damn perfect for me." He didn't think he'd said that out loud until he heard her breath hitch.

Her hair fell forward as he brought her mouth to his. "Roll me over, Jordan," she whispered. "I want to feel your power."

Her request tugged at his heart. He shifted them both to their sides, paused there for a moment, kissed her, then moved the rest of the way, sinking deeply into her as she lifted up and wrapped her legs around his hips.

And he held her gaze in between long, slow kisses, moving inside of her, feeling her match his steady rhythm as easily as if they'd done this for centuries. He finally slid his arm beneath her, tilted her hips up that extra bit so he could sink a tiny bit deeper, reach that spot he already knew was there, the one that made her gasp and tighten around him almost convulsively. The one he knew would take them both over the edge. But he held her there, for that one moment out of time, and looked into her eyes. "Grace…"

The look in her eyes mirrored his own feelings even as they both knew the reality of what they were doing to each other. And where it would lead them.

"With me," he said, pushing the rest of the way in.

"Always," he thought he heard her whisper, as she took him there and they both went over.

After what they had just shared, Grace knew that she

couldn't keep anything from him. Not even her darkest fear. She had to tell him.

He pulled her into his arms, tucked her against his chest.

"Jordan," she said, hesitation and trepidation clear in her voice.

He raised his head, his intense eyes totally focused on her.

"You were so brave tonight. I was awed by your courage to run into that fire and save the mayor and his family." Her throat closed and tears welled in her eyes. "It was something…I couldn't do."

He shook his head, his expression contradicting her. "I'm sure you've done it a thousand times."

"I have, without thought or fear, but now…now, I can't," she said, as sincere in that moment as she'd ever been.

"You can't?"

It was right there, right on the tip of her tongue, the truth. And the desire to tell him, to reveal that truth was so strong it actually made her ache. She took a steadying breath. She looked into his eyes and found exactly what she needed there. And then, it was suddenly quite easy. "I'm afraid of fire. I can't even smell smoke without getting this icy panic inside."

"I guessed that you were having a problem with it. I didn't know it was that pervasive."

"I can't do my job. I can't return to firefighting or to arson investigation. I don't think I would be effective." Tears slipped out of her eyes and he caught them with his thumbs.

"Grace, you've been through a terrible tragedy. You've lost people who meant a lot to you. You've got to give yourself time to heal."

"I feel like such an idiot. I should be handling this better."

"If it helps, I don't have the answers, either." He leaned back enough so she could look up into his face. "I just know I'd rather be here with you, handling this, than doing anything else. So I'm going with that for now. It can be that simple, Grace."

"Nothing in my life is that simple. Not now."

He traced the contours of her face with his thumbs. "It will be. We'll get there." He slid his hands down her arms and wove his fingers though hers, then held on.

For whatever reason, that undid her as nothing else could.

Her heart was still pounding, her mind still reeling, but his gaze and the way he held her hands, the size of his body, almost cradling hers, protecting her like a shield…it calmed her, soothed her in a way that at any other time would have had her scrambling to get away, as she didn't need any saving or soothing. But she'd be lying to herself if she said it didn't help her in that moment to find a center in the storm, to feel safely buffered for the first time in days. Weeks, even. Maybe forever.

"I'm not going anywhere," he said, "so stop trying to scare me off, okay?"

"You might be better off, Jordan."

He rose on his elbow and reached for her hand. "You are strong, Grace. I know that if anyone can handle everything you're dealing with now and somehow take care of every part of it and make all of it turn out right in the end, it's you. I have great respect for you. Or I wouldn't say it. I am not your white knight and I won't pretend to be. I'm just a man who wants to be with you.

We may not have had the same experiences, but we share the same emotions."

"I know we do, and because we do, it helps in understanding each other. What about you? Your fears?"

"At first I was concerned about you snapping and doing something irreversible like Dan. I don't think that anymore. I trust in your courage and your ability to handle what is happening to you. I have to come to terms with my own tendency to make snap judgments, as I did with you when we first met. It will make me a better agent and a better man."

He lifted their joined hands and dropped a kiss on one of her knuckles, then another.

She didn't know what to do with this, what to do with him.

He loosened his hold and turned her palm to his mouth. Then he kissed her there, before curling her fingers inward to hold on to it, another promise delivered and now sealed.

"To the rest of the world, we're two badasses who don't need anyone, okay?" he said, his voice a shade rougher now. "But right here, right now, you and I? We know differently."

She felt his fingers tighten slightly around hers, felt the warmth of his body, the strength that poured effortlessly out of him, doing nothing more than lying here with her. And she wanted to wrap herself in it, just for a moment or two, just long enough to draw strength from it and get her bearings back. Would that be so wrong? So horrible a thing?

Except it would come with a price. That price being expectation. If she took from him, he'd expect her to

give in return. Rightfully so. Could she do that? She
wasn't sure what was more terrifying—that she might
fail…or how badly she wanted to succeed.

"What do I offer you?" she asked, not realizing she'd
spoken out loud until he responded.

She shook her head. "An emotionally traumatized
woman who's stumbling around trying to get her
bearings? That seems like trouble to me."

He smoothed his hand through her hair. "You entice
me, spar with me, don't give an inch." He used their
joined hands to stroke his knuckles down the side of her
face, and his voice softened further. "You just came into
my life and I can't stop thinking about you. There's no
pulling punches with you, Grace. You'll tell me how it
is, not caring if it's what I want to hear or not."

"Damn straight. Can't be any other way."

His gaze grew serious. Which was quite terrifying
because she knew there was no hiding from him. He saw
right through her. It was like being naked at all times,
vulnerable at all times. It should unnerve her, but it was
also comforting. To know there was one person who got
her. Who would always get her. No matter what.

He kissed her knuckles again, then leaned in and
kissed the tip of her nose. Something about that simple
gesture, so sweetly innocent in its promise, so at odds
with the man she was coming to know, made tears spring
to her eyes again. "Jordan," she whispered shakily, "I
don't know what to do."

"You will. Give it time, Grace. You'll get yourself
back."

"Did you?"

"Almost. I think I'm almost there. Being with you
has made it easier somehow. I want to let go, but I can't
seem to yet."

"So time, huh?"

"Yeah."

Forty-five minutes later, lying in Jordan's arms, she should have been content. She should have been asleep, but she was too pent up to sleep. The case and its clues, connections and disconnections, rolled around in her head.

She signed heavily and tucked her arm beneath her head.

"What's wrong?"

"I can't sleep. I'm too...wound up. I'm sorry I'm keeping you awake."

"You're not. I can't sleep, either. What time is it?"

Grace turned to look at the clock. "It's midnight."

"What do you say we put in a few more hours on this case?"

Grace turned toward him. "I think that's a great idea. I just want all this to be over."

"I know."

"There's something nagging at me, but I can't figure out what it is. Every time I look at those photos Richard took at crime scenes, something...I don't know, keeps tickling my brain."

They rose and dressed. The streets were quiet, but the faint smell of smoke lingered in the air when they drove near the mayor's mansion. It brought back Grace's panic and she gripped the door handle. She'd finally admitted her fear, but she hadn't faced it. She hadn't beaten it and she was terrified that she never would. The job she wanted to do wouldn't be possible if she couldn't overcome this panic.

The municipal building parking lot was empty, as

expected, but when Grace looked up to the windows of the task force office, she noticed a soft glow.

"Did we leave a light on?"

Jordan glanced up and shrugged. "It's possible."

When they reached the office, Grace felt an urgency building in her. She walked over to her desk and opened the box. She handed Jordan one of the folders and took one for herself. Resolutely, she opened it and started reading.

Several hours later, her eyes burning, she leaned her head back. Richard had done a thorough job of cataloging all the fires he'd investigated and it was clear that the arsonist had been active for quite some time. Then that five-year dry spell. The dates seemed important to her, but she couldn't put her finger on what that meant.

When she pulled out the large file of pictures, Jordan put a hand on her arm. "I think it's time to call it quits for tonight. Let's get some sleep and we'll come back to it in the morning."

She put the file back on her desk. "All right. I think I can finally sleep."

"I'm going to make a pit stop before we head back. Power everything down and I'll be right back."

Jordan headed to the men's room. He quickly took care of his needs. As he emerged from the stall, he was brought up short. Tom Parker stood there, his stance in traditional cop mode: feet shoulder-width apart, arms extended with his very deadly police issued Smith & Wesson pointed directly at Jordan. Confusion pulled Jordan's brows into a frown. "Tom? What the hell?"

"You're a vigilant man. I'll give you that. The only times I've been able to get to Grace is through no fault of yours."

"You're Vulcan!"

Tom laughed low and mean. "Vulcan is an illusion, but it kept you and your task force busy, which was all that I needed." Tom gestured with his pistol. "Remove your firearm with two fingers and kick it over to me. Then facedown on the floor. Don't try anything. I don't want to have to shoot you."

Jordan complied. Tom was too far away from him for Jordan to effectively disarm him, and he couldn't help Grace if he was dead.

Tom tied Jordan's hands behind his back and then bound his feet. "Don't worry. It's like going to sleep. The smoke will get to you before the fire. It will be a peaceful death."

"You're going to let the fire do your dirty work." Jordan berated himself for not seeing through Tom. It was clear to him now that there were reasons he showed up every time Grace was in danger. Then it hit him like a lightning bolt out of the blue. There was no way he could have predicted what Tom would do, just as he couldn't have predicted what Dan would have done. He wasn't psychic and he couldn't read minds. No amount of training or experience would have done any good. All he could do was stay alive and find a way to help Grace.

Tom's voice was calm and soothing. "The fire will be a clean death, Jordan. Don't fight it."

Grace turned off the equipment and grabbed her purse. As she did, the corner of her bag connected with the file of photos and the folder tumbled off the edge of the desk and scattered across the floor.

Swearing softly, she bent down and stopped short. Tom was caught in the photo looking at a burning building, his cop uniform a dark blue against the flames.

In another, he was questioning witnesses and in yet another he was pulling crime scene tape to cordon off a crime scene. She knelt on the floor, shuffled through the pictures and the pieces fell into place. The five-year dry spell. It started the year Sara and Tom got married. Arsonists often changed their pattern or stopped altogether with a life change.

His veiled hostility toward her, his willingness to guard her. There was a reason he was captured in the tape from the hotel. He'd delivered the envelope right under their noses. Her blood froze, thinking about the times she'd been alone with him. He could have killed her so easily.

If he was the arsonist, why hadn't he?

She rose with one of the pictures in her hand and headed for the duty rosters. Richard had methodically dated every picture and she searched through the rosters. She found that for half the fires where he was present in the photos, he wasn't even on duty.

"Oh, God," she said softly. This meant that Tom had murdered Richard and had inadvertently killed his own wife.

"Looks like you've made a discovery, judging from the look on your face, Grace."

She jerked, her heart jumping in her chest, and looked up.

Tom Parker stood there holding a gun, and a self-satisfied smile curled his mouth as he watched her face change from discovery to fear.

While they faced off, the building rumbled and shook as massive explosions rocked the foundations.

"What have you done?"

"Nothing to worry about. We won't be disturbed by your lover, he's…tied up, I'm afraid. I can't believe out of all this, you end up with someone. There is no justice in the world."

Grace cried out, tears welling in her eyes and cascading down her cheeks. "Jordan," she whispered, her heart rending, shredded. "What would you know about justice, Tom?" she shouted.

"I know you're going to die, Grace. Now. There's nothing you can do about it."

Chapter 13

"Your time has finally run out, Grace. It's time to embrace the flames."

"Tom, you murdered Richard. You set up that fire to look like an arson to lure him over there and then you blew him up."

"I had to. He was getting way too close. He was questioning Sara about dates and times. She was getting agitated and worried. I could see her looking at me with suspicion. He made her look at me that way. He had to die. He was making me nervous and I started setting fires again."

"But you took great pleasure in filming it, Tom, in watching us die. You made no move to help us!"

"I wanted to see him suffer. I was surprised to see others involved. The bomb was designed specifically for him."

"Didn't you realize you murdered Sara? Your own wife?"

"No! I didn't know. She wasn't supposed to be on duty that day. I expected the firefighters to be gone. But he died too fast and all I was left with was the haunting image of my wife dying and you doing nothing! You weren't supposed to be there, either, Grace."

"But I was, Tom. I was there and I had to watch her die. Do you understand? I had to watch my best friend die."

"Shut up!" he said, hitting her across the face and knocking her back against the desk. The photos flew out of her hand and scattered across the floor.

The faint smell of smoke drifted to her and she tasted blood. She grabbed her throbbing face, the pain from the bruise on her chin flaring up.

Tom laughed, but it wasn't a normal laugh. It was high-pitched and a bit desperate, chilling her.

"Don't you get it? I made up Vulcan just to throw you off. Keep you busy while I planted evidence to frame that bastard Lyons. He's just as much to blame as the mayor. Both of them cheapskates. If they had replaced those SCBAs, Sara would be alive right now. This is your fault, too. You should have saved her. Isn't that your duty?"

Faced with a question she'd agonized over since Sara had died, Grace felt anger congeal inside her gut. "Yes, Tom, it was my duty to save her, but the truth of the matter is I couldn't. But I'm not the one who killed Sara. You killed her, and the guilt I feel from that day has tortured me for months. But I need to place the blame where it belongs, and that's on your shoulders. Sara's dead because of you, Tom."

And she knew the words were true. If Grace could have, she would have saved her friend, but she hadn't caused the fire that ended Sara's life. Sara's husband had.

Tom howled an eerie, inhuman sound that rumbled from his chest and burst out of him in a rush of sheer agony. And as the sound died away, Grace heard an even more chilling one.

The crackle of flames.

Jordan rolled over. Tom had tied his wrists together very tightly. With some agile maneuvering, however, Jordan wiggled until he was able to work his hands to the front. He worked at them, but it was painstakingly slow. He swore under his breath, his blood pumping in urgency. He had to get free. He had to get to Grace.

Tom grabbed Grace by the hair and pulled her over to the stairs. "You hear that?" he said. "You see those flames licking at the walls, consuming everything in their path? That's pure beauty there. You look at it and know that it will soon consume you."

"Let go," she cried, kicking at him, but his hand only tightened in her hair. The smoke was thickening, acrid and burning. Her eyes were tearing as she struggled. Tom flung her away from him.

She hit the floor hard and for a moment was stunned. Tom began to stalk her, this time his laughter sinister, his dark eyes trailing over her as if he was envisioning her on fire, her skin burning.

Then, through smoke-stinging eyes, she blinked. A shadow moved to the right of Tom in the direction of the restrooms. Jordan! He jumped at Tom and tackled him to the ground.

The gun flew from Tom's hand as he twisted and turned to strike at Jordan. They struggled. Jordan, using his bound hands clenched into fists, battered Tom's face in quick succession.

The fire billowed up the stairs, igniting the walls, the heat intense. Grace scrambled away from it in blind panic. Choking on smoke, she tried to keep the two men in view. Frantically she searched for the gun.

Tom delivered a hard blow to Jordan's chin and the impact drove him back. Debris rained down from the ceiling as a loosened ceiling tile crashed onto Jordan's head. He fell to the floor and didn't move.

"Jordan!" Grace yelled, renewing her search for the gun. Finally she saw it and she dived for it. Tom saw it at the same time. With a malicious grin, he leaped.

Grace got to it first. As her hand closed around the grip, everything seemed to slow. The fire hung suspended and it was as if Grace watched it in slow motion. She knew it. Knew its properties, knew its behavior. It was her sworn enemy and she looked into the face of her fear and didn't falter.

Tom's hand closed around the barrel and they grappled for control. An explosion rent the air and Tom staggered back, blood blossoming and soaking the front of his shirt. He looked down and staggered another step backward, clutching at his chest. Wordlessly he looked at her, and then he tumbled down the stairs and directly into the flames.

There was one horrible, nerve-scraping scream that assaulted her ears, then nothing but the encroaching flames.

She dropped the gun, her stomach jumping with nerves and reaction. She crawled over to Jordan, touching his face, shaking him. "Jordan. Wake up."

Jordan groaned and when his eyes fluttered open, she was never more thankful for that intense, if slightly unfocused, gaze.

"Grace... Tom?"

"He's dead. We've got to get out of here or we're next." He went to stand and she pushed him back down. "No. Stay down. Air is better down here."

"The fire escape is this way. Follow me," he said.

As she crawled, keeping Jordan in view, she pulled her cell phone out of her bag and dialed Mike. After giving him the details, she was brought up short by Jordan. He disappeared.

"Jordan?"

Fresh air wafted across her face and Jordan materialized out of the smoke and pulled her to her feet.

"Let's get out of here," he said. Together they exited the building.

"Didn't I say we had to stop meeting like this?" Smitty said as he treated Grace's minor burns and administered oxygen, again. They had used the fire escape to get free of the building and Grace released Jordan's bound hands.

She pulled down the mask. "This is the last time. I promise."

He reset the mask and smiled. "No talking."

Her attention shifted to Mike. The chief was in his element as he barked orders and directed the firefighters under his command. She could see that Mike was going to be just fine. That gave her a lot of satisfaction. They had both been emotionally scarred by that fateful day.

Now Grace had a totally different perspective. A few minutes later, Smitty released them.

An officer approached them and took them to the police station. After another hour of questions and explanations to the mayor and the police, Jordan and Grace were allowed to go back to the hotel. A patrol car dropped them off as the red of dawn tinged the horizon and the sun started to rise.

In their hotel room, they both decided on a shower to wash away the soot and smoke. As the water cascaded down on them, Grace wrapped her arms around him and said, "Thank you."

"For what?"

"For supporting me, for trying to convince me that Sara's death wasn't my fault, for telling me to let go of my guilt. I want to put all this behind us. I want to live, Jordan."

In his arms she found herself, found that her heart beat with life and need and want. Found that all the pain, all the agony, melted away in the deep depths of Jordan's eyes.

"I do, too, Grace. In all this I somehow have let go, too. In the wake of your courage I found my own way back."

Tears trailed down her cheeks as she touched his mouth with her fingertips. Their lips met as they each moved toward the other. A soft kiss that soon changed into something else.

She was pliant in his arms, thankful for his strength, his guidance, his support of her.

He was both gentle and urgent, making her feel cosseted and desired at the same time. He tucked his hips against hers and pulled her thighs up over his hips, pinning her to the wall. "Grace..." he murmured against her lips.

His eyes were such a breathtaking shade of blue, she'd never seen him this intense, which was saying something. And it was all because of her. A heady rush raced through her.

"I love you, Jordan."

She wanted—no, needed—him to know she was a true partner for him. In every way. And this was only the beginning of how she wanted to show him.

That feeling, that need, was thrilling and she felt no trepidation, no fear. Just as she'd embraced the fire and faced her fear, she could see nothing but a bright future for them.

"I love you, Grace, more than you can imagine."

"I can imagine a lot," she said, laughing against his mouth.

"Hold on to me, sweetheart."

She didn't hesitate to comply with his demand. She dug her fingers into his heavily muscled shoulders and locked her ankles more tightly behind him as he eased back from the wall, leaving her leaning back so he could angle her hips upward...and thrust. His broad palms covered her hips, guiding her down onto him. She arched, moaned, and when he began to move faster, she gasped at the intense pleasure.

What she felt was the irrevocable bond they had forged, a union like no other.

She gave herself over to him, reveled in his shuddering release, tightening around him.

Later, they lay entwined on the bed. "I've got a truly inspired idea," he said.

"What's that?" she replied drowsily.

"Hmm, I think I'll surprise you. I did promise to show you some fun."

"Yes, you did. Time to pay up."

* * *

The breeze off the ocean ruffled her hair as her feet stepped onto the sun-warmed deck. She could see him sitting on the beach, the sun glinting off his dark hair. No suits for him, just a naked, broad back and a pair of gray cotton shorts.

Grace moved forward, loving the feel of the flimsy, pink flowered sundress she'd slipped on over her nakedness.

This exclusive resort with a private beach was certainly inspired, she thought.

"Hey, there," she said by way of greeting. He turned and his eyes tracked her progress. She saw the love there, the admiration. Grace was content and she was sure it showed in every line of her body as she moved fluidly toward him.

"What are you doing out here all alone?"

"I was watching the sun rise, thinking of you."

"Mmm, I like that."

He tugged on her hand and she dropped down into the hot sand. She settled into his arms as easily as the waves crawled to shore.

"No regrets?" he asked.

"No, going back to being a firefighter feels immensely right. I want to save people, Jordan, not arrive after the fact when it's too late. And you?"

"Leaving the ATF to take Richard's job seems right, too. It's some big shoes to fill, but I intend to do my best and my new partner's name is Chloe."

"Your new partner is a dog."

"Now, that's no way to talk about her."

Grace laughed. "She's a Labrador Retriever and literally a dog. The chief is very proud that they now have a bona fide accelerant-sniffing canine."

Jordan nuzzled her neck and chuckled. Finally, he raised his head. "I have found that I've not only fallen in love with you, Grace, but I've also fallen in love with La Rosa."

Rubbing her cheek against his, she murmured, "I love you, too, Jordan."

A spark ignited along her skin, fueled by his touch. Those words on her lips sounded so right to her.

* * * * *

ROMANTIC
SUSPENSE

COMING NEXT MONTH

Available May 31, 2011

#1659 ENEMY WATERS
Justine Davis

#1660 STRANGERS WHEN WE MEET
Code Name: Danger
Merline Lovelace

#1661 DESERT KNIGHTS
Bodyguard Sheik by Linda Conrad
Sheik's Captive by Loreth Anne White

#1662 THE CEO'S SECRET BABY
Karen Whiddon

HRSCNM0511

REQUEST YOUR FREE BOOKS!
2 FREE NOVELS PLUS 2 FREE GIFTS!

Sparked by Danger, Fueled by Passion.

YES! Please send me 2 FREE Harlequin® Romantic Suspense novels and my 2 FREE gifts (gifts are worth about $10). After receiving them, if I don't wish to receive any more books, I can return the shipping statement marked "cancel." If I don't cancel, I will receive 4 brand-new novels every month and be billed just $4.24 per book in the U.S. or $4.99 per book in Canada. That's a saving of at least 15% off the cover price! It's quite a bargain! Shipping and handling is just 50¢ per book in the U.S. and 75¢ per book in Canada.* I understand that accepting the 2 free books and gifts places me under no obligation to buy anything. I can always return a shipment and cancel at any time. Even if I never buy another book, the two free books and gifts are mine to keep forever.

240/340 SDN FC95

Name	(PLEASE PRINT)
Address	Apt. #
City	State/Prov.	Zip/Postal Code

Signature (if under 18, a parent or guardian must sign)

Mail to the Reader Service:
IN U.S.A.: P.O. Box 1867, Buffalo, NY 14240-1867
IN CANADA: P.O. Box 609, Fort Erie, Ontario L2A 5X3

Not valid for current subscribers to Harlequin Romantic Suspense books.

Want to try two free books from another line?
Call 1-800-873-8635 or visit www.ReaderService.com.

* Terms and prices subject to change without notice. Prices do not include applicable taxes. Sales tax applicable in N.Y. Canadian residents will be charged applicable taxes. Offer not valid in Quebec. This offer is limited to one order per household. All orders subject to credit approval. Credit or debit balances in a customer's account(s) may be offset by any other outstanding balance owed by or to the customer. Please allow 4 to 6 weeks for delivery. Offer available while quantities last.

Your Privacy—The Reader Service is committed to protecting your privacy. Our Privacy Policy is available online at www.ReaderService.com or upon request from the Reader Service.

We make a portion of our mailing list available to reputable third parties that offer products we believe may interest you. If you prefer that we not exchange your name with third parties, or if you wish to clarify or modify your communication preferences, please visit us at www.ReaderService.com/consumerchoice or write to us at Reader Service Preference Service, P.O. Box 9062, Buffalo, NY 14269. Include your complete name and address.

Harlequin® Blaze™ brings you
New York Times *and* USA TODAY *bestselling author*
Vicki Lewis Thompson with three new steamy titles
from the bestselling miniseries SONS OF CHANCE

Chance isn't just the last name of these rugged
Wyoming cowboys—it's their motto, too!

Read on for a sneak peek at the first title,
SHOULD'VE BEEN A COWBOY

Available June 2011 only from Harlequin® Blaze™.

"THANKS FOR NOT TURNING ON THE LIGHTS," Tyler said. "I'm a mess."

"Not in my book." Even in low light, Alex had a good view of her yellow shirt plastered to her body. It was all he could do not to reach for her, mud and all. But the next move needed to be hers, not his.

She slicked her wet hair back and squeezed some water out of the ends as she glanced upward. "I like the sound of the rain on a tin roof."

"Me, too."

She met his gaze briefly and looked away. "Where's the sink?"

"At the far end, beyond the last stall."

Tyler's running shoes squished as she walked down the aisle between the rows of stalls. She glanced sideways at Alex. "So how much of a cowboy are you these days? Do you ride the range and stuff?"

"I ride." He liked being able to say that. "Why?"

"Just wondered. Last summer, you were still a city boy. You even told me you weren't the cowboy type, but you're…different now."

He wasn't sure if that was a good thing or a bad thing. Maybe she preferred city boys to cowboys. "How am I different?"

"Well, you dress differently, and your hair's a little longer. Your face seems a little more chiseled, but maybe that's because of your hair. Also, there's something else, something harder to define, an attitude…"

"Are you saying I have an attitude?"

"Not in a bad way. It's more like a quiet confidence."

He was flattered, but still he had to laugh. "I just admitted a while ago that I have all kinds of doubts about this event tomorrow. That doesn't seem like quiet confidence to me."

"This isn't about your job, it's about…your…" She took a deep breath. "It's about your sex appeal, okay? I have no business talking about it, because it will only make me want to do things I shouldn't do." She started toward the end of the barn. "Now, where's that sink? We need to get cleaned up and go back to the house. Dinner is probably ready, and I—"

He spun her around and pulled her into his arms, mud and all. "Let's do those things." Then he kissed her, knowing that she would kiss him back, knowing that this time he would take that kiss where he wanted it to go. And she would let him.

Follow Tyler and Alex's wild adventures in
SHOULD'VE BEEN A COWBOY
Available June 2011 only from Harlequin® Blaze™
wherever books are sold.

♦ Harlequin®

SPECIAL EDITION

Life, Love and Family

LOVE CAN BE FOUND IN THE MOST UNLIKELY PLACES, ESPECIALLY WHEN YOU'RE NOT LOOKING FOR IT...

Failed marriages, broken families and disappointment. Cecilia and Brandon have both been unlucky in love and life and are ripe for an intervention. Good thing Brandon's mother happens to stumble upon this matchmaking project. But will Brandon be able to open his eyes and get away from his busy career to see that all he needs is right there in front of him?

FIND OUT IN
WHAT THE SINGLE DAD WANTS...

BY *USA TODAY* BESTSELLING AUTHOR
MARIE FERRARELLA

AVAILABLE IN JUNE 2011
WHEREVER BOOKS ARE SOLD.

Harlequin Presents®

brings you

USA TODAY *bestselling author*

Lucy Monroe

with her new installment
in the much-loved miniseries

Royal Brides

Proud, passionate rulers—
marriage is by royal decree!

Meet Zahir and Asad—two powerful, brooding sheikhs
and masters of all they survey. They need brides,
and marriage in their kingdoms is by royal decree!

Capture a slice of royal life in this enthralling sheikh saga!

Coming in June 2011:

FOR DUTY'S SAKE

Available wherever
Harlequin Presents® books are sold.

www.eHarlequin.com

HP12993